Remedy and Ruins

Astoria Wright

Faerie Apothecary Mysteries
Book 2

Remedy and Ruins

Published by Novelwright Press, LLC
http://www.novelwright.com

Cover Art by Viyiwi
www.fiverr.com/viyiwi

Editing by 529 Books
https://www.529books.com
Editors: Lisa Cerasoli and Adrian Muraro

Table of Contents

Chapter 1

Pumpkins and Premonitions

The pumpkin spice tea warmed Carissa Shae to her core. She pulled her long sleeves over her thumbs and cradled the cup in her hands, relishing the heat. Her pink nose made her hair seem redder, and the orange sweater didn't help.

The contrast of the crisp fall weather and the steamy holiday tea invited her to stay in the garden a little longer. From her seat on the patio, she had a perfect view of Mount Vale, the most mysterious feature of Moss Hill—mysterious, that is, to any human who was not half-fae. All Mossies, as the residents of Moss Hill referred to themselves, knew that the western mountain was home to elves and sidhe and several other kinds of faerie people, yet being human and never having seen the fae village, they were distant enough to view the mountain with awe. Still, at the right time, in the right season, at just the right angle, walking through the forest up the mountain could lead to the Otherworld.

Today fit those conditions perfectly. Since this was the first year that Moss Hill had fully embraced travelers to the island,

Carissa wondered whether any of the tourists would be fool hearty enough to try to enter the woods there. She hoped not.

Though the fae had not opposed Mayor Belkin's plan to increase tourism and understood the humans' need to boost the economy, non-fae venturing into their area was not desired by any of the larger faerie people—especially the sidhe. They might have looked the most human, except for slightly above normal heights and pointier ears than any elf's, but they were the least welcoming to outsiders. This was possibly because of their role as protectors of the Otherworld, a job they took with deadly-serious devotion. Carissa shuddered, recalling her last encounter with the oldest of the faerie races.

Her grandmother joined her in a thick, button-down mauve sweater with a teacup and saucer in one hand and the Friday newspaper in the other. Her cheeks held a rosy glow against her strangely young-looking face as she adjusted her glasses. Her short, grey hair stayed perfectly in place as a gust of wind caused a tremble to go down her spine. "It's too cold to be sitting out here."

"I like watching the leaves change color," Carissa replied, gazing at the few trees in her garden, then past the countryside to the forest of Mount Vale.

"They changed color a month ago. They're falling off the trees now." Nan took a seat on the white wood patio chair under the sea-green umbrella. She shifted her gaze to follow her granddaughter's. "Are you missing them?"

"Who?"

"Who else? Dorian of Vale," she exaggerated the name, "and my whimsical daughter."

"Dad and Mom? No, they're having fun in…." She forgot where they'd gone this time but shrugged it off. "They're coming back in a few more weeks anyway."

"Then what's got you down?"

"Nothing." She knew as soon as the word was out of her mouth that she'd missed the mark in trying for a nonchalant attitude. Nan sipped her tea and said nothing, for which Carissa was grateful.

Another moment of calm passed. The nature faeries must have still been asleep. Not a branch, twig, or leaf was moving.

Nan buttered the toast Carissa had set out earlier and sipped tea as she read the morning paper. She grumbled and read aloud, "Mayor Belkin Sets Record for Tourism and Boosts Moss Hill Economy."

Nan shook her head in disapproval. A strand of short silver hair fell to the side of her rimless glasses. Carissa appreciated that Nan wore them up to the bridge of her nose unlike the stereotypes of librarians who let them slip down too far when they read. She loved that her face still held more than a trace of her youth. If Cari's half-elf genes hadn't blessed her with longevity, at least she hoped she'd inherited her grandmother's resilience toward age.

"The mayor's a smart man when it comes to money, but that's about all. Cari, I tell you, half the problems in Moss Hill are that man's doing."

"What do you mean, Nan? He didn't cause the Leanansidhe to appear or send the pixies or the hobgoblin." Carissa believed that truly rational arguments could not be out-reasoned, but she waited for Nan's reasoning. If she knew one thing about Nan, it was that her logic was impeccable. She never made an argument that was not categorically, undeniably true. It just took some people more time to realize it than others.

"I'm not saying he plucked them out of the earth and placed them here, but what he did was just as bad."

The warmth of the last sip of tea coursed down Cari's throat. She set the cup down, secretly wishing for more.

"Which is what?"

"He *advertised*." Nan plunged her index finger into the paper.

"The increase in tourism. I know." Carissa sighed. "I've thought about that too. But the fae council agreed to it."

"Why is that?" Nan asked. At first, Cari thought the question was rhetorical, but Nan tilted her head like a school teacher waiting for a pupil to think of the answer.

"I don't know," Carissa's tone piqued. She hadn't generally been a surly student, but it was too early in the morning to jump through mental hoops.

"Perhaps you should find out." Nan took her last bite of bread and made that her final word. She turned the newspaper page. She'd made her point, but Cari wasn't sure what to make of it.

Carissa left her seat, kissed Nan on the forehead, and said goodbye. She lifted her plate and cup and went inside. Closing the sliding door, she walked to her left and placed the dishes in the sink, then looked out the window to see if the pint-sized nature faerie in the hanging basket was still asleep. Chaos, aptly named for such a troublesome sprite, made no peep, so Cari didn't wake her.

She knew the moment the nature faerie woke she'd smell the lingering aroma of the pumpkin spice tea—which had become a fast favorite of hers—and demand that Nan make more by fluttering around the cabinets and pounding her little hands where she knew they kept the tea. Carissa set out a new tea bag beside the kettle to avoid damage to the cabinet. She grabbed her grey coat, chartreuse purse, her bag of weekly fresh picked herbs, and her keys, then she walked through the hallway.

At the sitting room, one step down off the side of the front door, the window sat partly open. The curtain danced in the breeze. Cari hadn't realized they'd left it open the night before. She stepped down and leaned over the sofa, looking outside. All was quiet. A few leaves drifted in the wind, the ones in the trees rattled. Not a person in sight. Carissa didn't like it. It was like the calm before the storm. Yet, she had no idea why she felt that way.

No, that wasn't true. It all had to do with a simple note she'd found tucked away in the bookcase yesterday: one from a woman named Raven Corvus. She tried to forget about it

4

by stuffing it in an old book, but books were the worst place to hide messages one didn't want to read.

The appearance of a note and a nature faerie, Chaos, four months ago on the steps of her natural pharmacy, the Seelie Tree Apothecary, had disrupted her life. "*Fae are coming that you would rather not meet,*" it had read. Dark faeries, the unseelie, invading Moss Hill—that's what the note implied. She thought it was just the once when they'd banished a banshee. Then the Leanansidhe turned up along with a hobgoblin. She hadn't even connected the note with their arrival. Now she felt it wasn't a coincidence that more than one dangerous fae had come to town. The letter had warned her, after all. It begged the question, what was coming next?

For that matter, why were they coming at all? Cari's mind repeated Nan's words, *he advertised*. Tourism had been good for the shops, and Cari had met some interesting new people. She wanted to like the change but feared that it marked the beginning of trouble.

Carissa closed the window, retraced her steps to the hall, and faced the bright red door again, opening it to meet the day. Only after she stepped outside did she realize how tightly she was clutching the keys. Cari nearly hugged them to her chest. Turning to face the shiny silver handle, she pulled the door shut. No one in Crescent Circle, in fact probably no one in Moss Hill, ever locked their doors. Now, she felt compelled to do so. She didn't know why her fingers inserted the key, why her wrist turned the lock, but when her hand came away, she felt a sense of relief. Nan and the sprites would be safe.

The bicycle ride to the shop, which usually relaxed her, did not even register into conscious awareness. She mechanically pedaled through the damp, swerving streets, past the community garden of her neighborhood. They were trying for pumpkins and squash this season, and the haze of oranges and yellows meant they were succeeding. On the long stretch of neatly cultivated crops along Greenfield Road, Cari passed the fall vegetation with little notice of how everything was in bloom. She barely registered the scent of rain and the feel of it drizzling over her skin. The greener than green vibrancy of the plant life renewed by the showers ordinarily reenergized her soul. The sight was lost on her today.

Given the tense feeling wrapping itself around her insides, she should have been hyperaware of her surroundings. Instead, she didn't even see the big black dog in the road before it was right in front of her. She pulled at the brakes of her bicycle, and her feet flew away from the pedals as she nearly crashed into the animal. Using a bit of her elf-magic, purely by instinct, she was able to jump off at the last minute and throw her arms out to stop the bicycle from sliding into the poor pet.

"Oh my gosh." Her heart raced. "Are you all right?" She lost her breath looking into the dog's red eyes. This was no pet. This was the barguest: the Black Dog of Death.

She'd seen it once before when a Mossie had died. It was not a good omen. The otherworldly dog, with its canine teeth, large frame, black-as-night fur, and eyes glowing like fire, stood in the road long enough for her to be sure of what she was seeing. Then, it trotted off onto the path that diverged from the corner of Greenfield and Gorse up to the way into Vale. The mountain took on an eerie hue this foggy morning. It wasn't just her imagination. The otherworldly vibes were strong today.

She picked up the green purse and the sealed bag of herbs strewn across the ground. Tossing them back into the basket, she took her place back on the seat and whispered to herself, "This is a terrible idea."

Then she set her eyes on the path where the dog had disappeared into the mists and cautiously rode up the trail. She strained to make out the black form until she came to the place where the roads forked again: left to the Vale woods or right toward Fairfield castle. *Where could the dog have gone?*

She'd heard stories about people seeing the barguest around the castle grounds. Sure enough, she thought she saw a shadow at the entrance of the castle to her right. On the other hand, she was sure she'd heard the wind howling to her left. Her decision was made the next second when she heard a shriek. It was followed by the wavering words wafting through the air, "G-Get back! H-Help!"

Carissa pedaled into the woods as fast as her feet could take her. She'd have used her elf-light magic to go even faster, but it turned out she didn't need to go that far. Only a few feet in, she saw a man stumbling and stubbing his toes on the rocks and tree roots around him.

He was definitely not a Mossie. The way he was dressed, in his green overcoat and faded khaki pants, he looked like he was on an expedition. His reddish-brown hair waved wildly as he jumped about. Most obviously marking him a tourist was the camera around his neck. It flung and hit him in the chest on the last jump.

"Ouch!" He grabbed the camera and rubbed his sternum. Then he waved awkwardly again at the air. "Give those back! I can't see!"

Cari's face tightened to stern disapproval. Not one, but four duergars appeared and disappeared around the trees. The minuscule male faeries' lambskin coats and moleskin pants blended with the scenery. Dirt covered their faces. Their moss hats completed their camouflage, but it was their magic cloaks, allowing them to constantly shift between the human and fae realms, that made them invisible to all but faerie eyes. The two-feet-tall, dwarf-like faeries threw the man's glasses between themselves, cackling as they enjoyed their game of keep-away. Carissa set her bicycle against a tree and marched up. The duergars fancied themselves the guardians of faerie paths, but this was too much.

"Ahem, stop that!"

"Wh-who's there?" The man swished his head about him.

Carissa put a fist on her hip and held one hand out in front of her. The duergar holding the glasses dropped his head. He appeared beside her and grouchily handed her the frame, not without a snort of disapproval before the four scampered back into the woods.

"H-hello? Wh-who are you?" The man squinted at Cari.

"I'm Carissa Shae." She walked over and handed him his glasses.

"Reginald Smith," he said, readjusting the frames to his face. The moment he could see clearly again, he circled the area. "Did you see them?" he asked. He picked up his camera and took at least half a dozen snapshots. He might have included Carissa, but she put a hand in front of her face and blinked in the flashing light.

"See who?" Carissa asked. She tried her best to look innocent, keeping her face as mild as possible even though she was properly annoyed.

"There were some creatures here." He touched his glasses' frames like they were binoculars. "I don't know exactly, but I heard a shriek and some laughing. And something snatched my glasses."

Carissa noticed the scratch on the side of his head.

"You're sure it wasn't just a branch that knocked your glasses off?" She pointed to her forehead. Reg touched his temple and winced.

"I don't think so. These woods are supposedly infested with supernatural beings."

Carissa grimaced at the word "infested." It was possibly the least polite way she'd ever heard a human refer to a faerie.

Reginald adjusted his glasses again. "What are you doing out here?"

"I was on my way to work and I heard you shouting." Cari kept her cool. Her elf-light magic was at risk of giving her away if she strayed too far from the truth. Both parts of her statement were facts, even if she left out the events in the middle.

"You work in the woods?" Reg did a full turn as he surveyed the area.

"I work down the road." She pointed back toward Greenfield.

"And you heard me all the way up here? You must have very good hearing."

Blood rushed to the tips of Cari's pointed ears as he studied them. This human was inquisitive, to say the least.

"What are you doing out here anyway?" Carissa asked.

He stood tall and said with ridiculous confidence, "I am a sleuth solving a mystery."

"Really? What mystery is that?"

He hunched forward. "I think you know."

She recoiled. "I really don't."

He studied her a moment longer, hitched his glasses again with his index finger on the nose bridge and began walking down the trail. "Never mind. I just have to gather more evidence. I'll get my answers another way."

Carissa grabbed her bicycle and followed. Something tugged on the hem of her pant leg. There was Noz, a short goblin-looking creature, a bugul-noz. To most humans, he appeared to be a hairy, scary little man, but Cari knew him as the kindest old fae in Vale. He lived alone, as even the fae weren't always the nicest about his looks.

"I'm sorry, Cari. I made the shrieking sound. I couldn't help it. He scared me. I wasn't expecting to see a human 'round here. Do you think he saw me?" Noz asked in a low voice.

"No," Carissa whispered. "Go back home, Noz. It's all right."

He turned and sluggishly blended back into the trees.

Carissa caught up with the tourist while pushing her bicycle through the woods.

"Where are you going?" she asked.

"Back to town." He kept onward like he was on a mission. She'd have gotten back on the bicycle and ridden away, but she had a feeling he was someone she and her fellow Mossies might need to keep an eye on.

"I'll walk with you."

He glanced out the corner of his eye. "Do you all bicycle around here?"

"Not all of us. I'm just not partial to cars myself. Why?"

"I didn't see a car rental place anywhere in town."

"We have taxis."

"I'm not partial to taxis." He parroted her words back to her. Reginald's stomach growled loud enough that Carissa could hear it.

Cari bit her lip. This man was strange, but what unnerved her even more was the sidelong glances he kept giving her. She needed to allay his suspicions. Kindness, she decided, was her best tactic.

"If you haven't had breakfast—"

"Nice try. I know all about your tricks. When an elf offers you food, don't eat it. It'll get you stuck in the Otherworld."

Carissa's eyebrows shot up. He was quoting it like a rule from a book, but she'd never heard anything so ludicrous. She almost wanted to argue that it was untrue and offensive, but then she'd be admitting she was an elf.

"I know all about seelie and unseelie faeries, about elves and sidhe and brownies and goblins and powries and red caps and blue caps and leprechauns and—" He listed about twenty fae types, some of which she'd never heard of before.

All she could do was stare at him, dumbfounded. No one outside of Moss Hill had ever called her an elf before. Non-Mossies would never even have expected it.

"I was going to suggest a bakery called Gooseberry. It's just around the corner."

He didn't respond. Upon closer inspection, she realized he had goosebumps on his arms. Was he scared of her? She decided the best way to calm him down was to keep talking so he'd see her as a regular person and let go of the idea she was an elf.

"Or there's the Old Main, that's a restaurant in the center of town. Or we could do Second Street Pub down by the marina."

Remedy and Ruins

When they arrived on the corner of Greenfield and Gorse, the black cassock of the local priest came into view.

"Good morning, Father Quinn," Carissa called out. She tried her best to seem normal and friendly to Reginald's seemingly suspicious nature. It was easy to be neighborly with Father Quinn.

"Good morning, Carissa." He closed his umbrella.

"Father, this is Reginald Smith. He's visiting Moss Hill from—I'm sorry, where did you say you were from?"

Reg's mouth opened and lingered there as if deciding if it was safe to say. "England," he finally said. "London, England."

"And what do you think of Moss Hill, my good fellow?" the priest asked.

Cari cringed and thought of John Goodfellow, but Father Quinn might not have known about that particular visitor to Moss Hill, so she could hardly blame him for his choice of words.

"I'm still deciding," Reginald said. "Tell me, Father, what do you know of the town's history?"

"Quite a lot, my boy. What particular questions did you have?"

"I'll start with elves."

"Elves?" The priest's tone was as surprised as Cari had been. "What about them?"

"Are there any? Here in Moss Hill, I mean?"

This put the priest in the exact spot as Cari. Carissa couldn't lie because her elf-magic would begin a faint glow as her heart beat faster. Father Quinn couldn't lie because, well, she assumed his priestly office wouldn't warrant such a thing as false speech.

"Who of us can say what things exist around us without our knowledge?" Father Quinn retorted.

Carissa breathed a sigh of relief as Reginald and the priest walked in front of her. As Father Quinn was off to Gooseberry, he'd no doubt set the tourist right by the end of breakfast. Cari was glad the ominous start to the day was changing. She thought of the dreadful feeling she'd had earlier and the barguest she'd seen.

On the corner of Greenfield and Gorse, she twisted around to take another look at the castle. There was still a misty cloud hanging over it. *Why had the barguest gone there this morning? Had the castle been its destination?*

Chapter 2

October Occasions

The shadows over the Seelie Tree Apothecary darkened as it started to rain.

"Inside!" Maren's voice cut through Carissa's thoughts. She looked over to see her assistant and best friend running from the bakery to the building next door. Carissa dashed alongside Maren to the door. She retrieved her purse from the basket only to realize that she'd held her keys the whole ride down to the store.

"Oh, for goodness sake." Maren grabbed the keys out of Carissa's hand and thrust open the door. "Quick, get in!" Carissa obeyed, realizing that a full-blown torrent had begun outside. Maren closed the door in exasperation. "Didn't you notice the rain?"

"I'm sorry, I didn't." Carissa turned and looked out the window. "It's really pouring." Maren had already disappeared in the back room and come out with a roll of paper towels in hand. She ripped off a few and tossed the roll to Carissa while patting down her hair and shoulders. Carissa followed suit.

"Well, at least we made it inside in time to avoid getting completely drenched." Maren looked at the floor and pouted. "We'll have to mop before we open the shop today."

"Oh, the herbs!" The mention of the apothecary shop opening snapped Carissa back into full awareness. "They're outside on the bicycle."

Maren took the paper towel and headed back to the storeroom. "Leave it for now, the weather's so fickle. It'll stop raining by the time we clean up." She re-emerged, mop in hand.

Carissa, back in her usual demeanor, smirked and placed her hands on her hips. "Do I run this place or do you?"

Maren shook her head but failed to conceal the smirk. "We've already had this discussion. I don't want to be a partner. I'm not crazy enough to want that kind of responsibility."

Since the events of past months, with Maren being controlled by a leanansidhe and manipulated by a hobgoblin to try to take over the shop, Carissa suspected that underneath it all, Maren might really want a partnership in the store. Maren assured her more than once that that was not the case. Carissa didn't mind it either way. The truth was, Maren was one heck of an assistant, and she couldn't see running the shop without her.

Carissa traveled through the central row of shelves lined with herbal tonics, vitamin supplements, and homeopathic remedies to the back counter, then turned right and curved around the corner to the back hall. The wind knocked against the back door, a familiar noise that put her on edge for some reason. Turning to the little room on the left, she switched on the light and entered. She hung her purse on the coat hanger by Maren's and turned on the computer.

She did her best not to check work email at home. A separation between business and personal life was necessary for a healthy balance, which made it curious when an email from Tilly Brier popped onto her screen. The library assistant and aspiring actress was a member of Nan's literary society, poetry club, and just about every arts organization in town. She wasn't a close friend, not someone with whom Cari had clicked and certainly not someone with whom the Seelie Tree Apothecary would need to do business. Tilly's email was a subscription of some kind, containing a link to something called *Mossie Musings*. She clicked the link. A blog came up with articles written by none other than Tilly herself.

Carissa exited the screen and rose from the chair. She was pretty sure she knew who'd signed them up for the email updates. No matter how many times she told her not to use the shop's email—or internet connection, for that matter—for anything other than official business, Maren never seemed to follow that rule.

"Maren?" Carissa exited the doorway and folded her arms. She leaned against the wall. "Did you sign up the Seelie Tree's email for Tilly's blog?"

"Ooh, does she have a new post up?"

Maren turned on the tablet that was supposed to only be used as a register and opened the email to scour the *Mossie Musings* website. Carissa's hands dropped to her sides, and her shoulders slumped. Maren was oblivious to her annoyance, as usual. Making her way beside her assistant, Cari tried to reiterate her point.

"You know the email's not for personal use...."

A word caught her eye as Maren scrolled through several new posts. "Magnus MacLir to Visit Moss Hill" read the heading. The word disappeared when Maren clicked on a different article.

"Look at this," Maren said. "Gooseberry's holding a pumpkin carving contest for the All Hallows' Eve celebrations. The theme is 'Perilous Pumpkins.' I wonder if the town could do a pumpkin themed baking contest this year to go along with it. You know, use the pumpkin's insides as well as the outside? I've been wanting to test my baking skills against Hattie's and, really, who doesn't like pumpkin themed desserts?"

"Go back," Cari ordered, still staring at the screen. She didn't mean to be dismissive, but Maren was only sore because her sister, Hattie, won the last competition years ago and they hadn't had one since.

Cari waved a hand at the screen as if she could will it back by magic. If her elf-light could work on technology, she probably would have done so. So far, her magic only made modern devices malfunction.

"Back where?" Maren clicked the back button even as she asked.

"There." Carissa pointed to the article.

"Magnus MacLir? Who's that?"

"*MacLir*, Maren, remember?" Cari said as if stressing the name would provoke the memory.

Maren obliged. "MacLir Industries, the company John worked for, the one doing the renovations on Fairfield Castle. He's the owner."

After she'd said it, she realized the effect bringing up John's name had on her friend. Maren looked down at the floor. A flicker of pain passed over her face. Cari's own lips pulled back in regret.

"Sorry, I didn't mean to bring him up." Carissa's hand went to her friend's shoulder.

Maren walked away, pretending to wipe the counter, swiping vainly at imagined crumbs.

"I guess I blocked that out of my memory a bit," she said.

Carissa understood. Breakups were difficult enough— almost getting killed took it to a whole 'nother level. In moments like this, she realized how strong Maren really was to be dealing with something like that and not be a total wreck.

The weather outside rattled the door and the sound pulled Carissa and Maren out of their sullen silence. The howling wind was accompanied by the sound of bells chiming. The pair turned their curious eyes to the door.

It was far too early for customers, but the old-fashioned bells above the door were swinging back and forth. Below them, Cameron Larke, recently appointed the liaison between fae and humans of Moss Hill, entered in a long coat and umbrella. Carissa looked at Maren. Neither of them had thought to lock the door, but Cameron was more than a customer. He was a friend, and based on Maren's mischievous grin as he entered, she clearly thought he and Cari were more than friends. That was a theory Carissa believed she had never given credence to.

"Hello, everyone!" he greeted. Had his shoulders grown broader or was it just the winter coat adding to an illusion? Or was he just more confident these days? He'd recently finished his online business degree, for which he'd spent untold hours at the library. Since he'd gone from chauffeur to the mayor's liaison with the neighboring people of Vale, he seemed to walk with a bit more pride. Whatever it was, Cari was glad to see him in such a chipper mood.

She winced as he went from dashing to disheveled, shaking his umbrella outside clumsily. He failed to put it in the stand by the door. Haphazardly wiping his feet on the mat, he trudged inside, the umbrella dripping along the way.

"I just cleaned that floor!" Maren grabbed the mop then stomped over to him. She took the light-green contraption out of his hand and put it in its proper place. Apparently not noticing Maren's scowl as she cleaned up his tracks, he continued on to the counter.

"Great news! I had to come to tell you first thing." He leaned his hip and elbow against the counter, talking to Carissa and Maren at the same time. "I had a meeting with the mayor and a few prominent citizens of Moss Hill, and we all agree that fae/human relations have been strained since...well, you know." He was referring to Miss Morgan's death, which happened in the store just two months prior. Her face drained of color at the mention of it. He continued, "So, I had an idea to host a celebratory party for All Hallows' Eve. Instead of having a party in the center of town, which few fae attend anyway, I thought we should have it in Fairfield Castle, *and*," he leaned in further, "we would have both fae and humans to decorate and organize the events."

Cam's waited eagerly for her and Maren's thoughts.

"All Hallows' Eve in an abandoned castle?" Maren said, joining them and setting the mop by the counter. "Sounds spectacular!"

Carissa wondered if she should say anything about the barguest. She wasn't even sure it had been going to the castle. It might have been there to warn her about Reginald. Reginald Smith: that was a whole other problem. She'd rather not jump to conclusions about either one without more information.

"Sure," Carissa agreed. "But—" Cari noted that Cam's lips dropped a little in anticipation. "I don't see how that'll bring more than a few extra fae."

The flashy-toothed smile returned. "It will, because," he held up a finger, "firstly, it matters how they're invited. We'll hold a meeting with the fae representatives to personally to spread the word among the faeries of Mount Vale."

"Good luck getting them to speak with you," Maren said.

Cameron turned toward the skeptical assistant and held up two fingers.

"We will get them to speak with us because, secondly, it matters who is involved in organizing the event and we still need a subcommittee leader in charge of decorating the castle."

"You have someone in mind?" Carissa asked.

"I have the perfect someone in mind." He grinned. Maren got it before she did, based on her chuckling. The two stood still on either side of the counter. Cameron held a long, expectant face.

Carissa sighed. "Oh no, Cam, you can't be serious."

"But I can." He pushed himself off the counter and held both hands open to her as if showcasing his point. "You're perfect for this, Carissa. Half-human, half-elf, you've saved the town twice now; everybody loves you."

"No, *no*," she stressed. "That is a horrible idea."

"The mayor thinks it's a great idea."

"I second that!" Maren said.

"No. Things have just gotten back to normal. I'm still restocking from the last equinox celebrations. I've got orders to fill."

"And excuses to make," Maren chided.

Carissa glared and put a hand on her hip. "I'd be crazy to want that kind of responsibility."

Maren placed both hands on the counter and practically stood on her tiptoes, beaming as she told Cam, "She's in. And you can count me in, too, as a helper."

"A helper for what?" The bell chimed, and a certain leprechaun dampened the floor again as he entered. He looked down and shook off his muddy shoes. Cari put a hand over her mouth, trying to contain a chuckle as her eyes darted to her assistant. As if on cue, Maren grabbed the mob and stormed over.

"Barnaby! Could you please use the mat outside before coming in? That's what it's there for! Honestly, why do I bother?"

The little man took off his hat and frowned. "Sorry, Maren, I wasn't thinking." If he'd wanted to prove his point, he could not have done it better than by wringing out his green cap to create a puddle where his shoes had muddied up the floor. He seemed to realize in the middle of it what he was doing. He froze and met Maren's gaze of death by shrinking in toward his shoulders, like a turtle trying to go back inside its shell. Barnaby walked up to the counter, smiling innocently as Maren got behind him with the mop.

Cam went back to leaning on the counter. "Cari, please, as a personal favor?" Cameron Larke had somehow retained his childhood puppy dog face and knew just when to use it to his advantage.

"What's this about a favor?" Barnaby pried.

Maren followed with the broom. Each time she swung it, Cari thought she'd tackle the leprechaun with it. But no, she finally lifted it off the floor and walked behind the counter to set it down again.

Maren answered Barnaby's question, apparently forgiving him for the mess. "Cameron wants her to be in charge of a committee to decorate the All Hallows' Eve celebration at the old Fairfield Castle."

"All Hallows' Eve at the castle?" Barnaby stroked his thick red beard.

Maren ignored his comment and leaned an elbow on the counter, facing Cari directly. "And it's not just a personal favor to Cam. It'll be good for you, too," Maren said.

"For me? Why?"

"Because you've been jumpy and uptight ever since the, um, you know." Carissa felt her skin crawl at the thought of the hobgoblin but kept listening. "I think it would be therapeutic to get out there with people and do something fun. You can't keep your head down and work all the time. It's not healthy."

Carissa pulled her lips taught between a grateful smile and an apologetic frown. She should have been giving Maren this speech. After all, she'd not only had her life threatened, but she'd had the worst break-up with a boyfriend anyone in town could imagine. Yet the boisterous brunette had gotten over the troubles of the past month better than anyone expected. With a cute round face, average height, and slim build, the blue-eyed, outgoing shop girl had a disposition that wasn't kept down for long. She might not be very confident, but her friends were more plentiful than Cari's and their carefree attitudes added to Maren's resilience. In addition to that, her sister was a counselor. No wonder she saw a chance at socializing on the planning committee as therapy.

"Therapeutic, yes." Barnaby twitched his head and gave his beard a tug. "Good distraction for a drunkard, too."

All three sets of eyes turned toward him. He took a full second to look up at the three taller individuals.

Cameron, who looked the most puzzled out of the three, was the first to speak. "Who are you talking about, Barn?"

Cari appreciated the skepticism in his voice with its subtle implication that Barnaby couldn't possibly have been talking about her. Which, of course, he couldn't have been.

"I think I know," Maren said. Her *tsk-tsk* clued Cari in as well.

"Oh, Barn, is Clancy at it again?"

Barnaby put his green cap back on and moved his chin up and down. "That cousin of mine is always making trouble."

"I'm sure it's not easy living in a wine cellar," Maren sympathized.

"Clurichauns love wine cellars—even the musty drabness of the places, they don't all steal the wine." Barnaby gave his haughty reply.

"The clurichaun who's always swiping from the vineyards?" Cam asked, seemingly oblivious to how insensitive that sounded. Cari grabbed his arm and gave it a squeeze, just enough for him to get the point. Cam turned a little red. "I mean, uh, I didn't realize Clancy was your cousin."

"Hmpf. Barely. A distant relative on my mother's side. He's in my store right now with a head-splitting headache, from you know what. Cari, do you have something for him?"

"Of course, Barn." Cari made her way around the counter to the shelves in the second row.

"Thanks," Barnaby called. He lifted his eyes and cocked his head to one side, using the counter to propel himself upwards to inquire from Cameron, "About that castle decorating committee, I think it would do a world of good for Clancy to be on it. It'd get him out of the wine cellar for a while, anyway. What do you say?"

Cam raised his voice for all to hear. "That's not really up to me. That's up to whoever leads the committee."

Carissa rounded the corner to see Cam smirking, his eyes wide in anticipation of her response.

"Not me, Cam, sorry." She handed the ginger-turmeric concoction to Barnaby. The leprechaun pulled out enough bills for the payment. She put them in the register and gave him his change.

Silent stares were aimed in her direction. They wouldn't relent now, or even if by some miracle they did, she'd be faced with moping and disappointed remarks from now until the holiday if she didn't give in.

"All right." The eye roll was completely ignored by everyone in the group until she put a finger up and added sharply, "I'll come to the meeting, but I'm only going to participate, not lead any subcommittees."

Cam's smile had a hint of some mischief that wasn't lost on Carissa. "No problem. They'll choose someone at the meeting," he said.

She gripped the counter. "It better be a fair election."

"Of course," Cam said, too innocently to be believed.

"I'm sure it will be," Maren said almost in unison. Now she aroused suspicion as well, or else Cari was just being paranoid.

Carissa pointed at Maren. "You're helping."

"I already volunteered," she said as if Carissa were slow.

Cam spun around and Cari swore there was a literal spring in his step as he opened the door. "First meeting is at the Second Street Pub at 5:00 p.m. Don't be late!" he called out, then he set off, most likely to tell the mayor the good news.

Barnaby, on whom subtle gestures were often lost, replied cheerfully that he and Clancy would be right on time. Then he tipped his hat, and he, too, left the apothecary shop with a bounding delight.

Maren walked past Cari to put away the mop in the back room, but she halted at the end of the counter to flash her pearly whites in her boss's direction. "You won't regret this," she said. Carissa had a strong feeling that she would regret it very much.

Chapter 3

Eavesdropping and Evil Eyes

The Second Street Pub bustled with more patrons than usual. Carissa arrived at the same time as Barnaby and Clarence, opening the glass door for the two shorter folks to walk in before her. The confused electric bell chimed twice as she opened it wider for a gentleman behind them.

"Wow, I've never seen it this busy before," Cari observed.

"It's the tourists. The pub's the closest restaurant to the marina. The visitors have been good for business," Barn said. He took his green cap off now that they were indoors and pointed at Clancy for him to do the same.

The clurichaun scowled and grabbed the red hat off his head as if it weighed a ton. "Good for business," he repeated in a bitter tone. His discolored teeth showed. "Bad for drinkin', I say." He fidgeted with the hat in his hands. "I'd rather have stayed in the cellar by myself."

"Only you're not by yourself." Barnaby pulled him out of the doorway so the man behind them could pass. "You got thrown out because you like to prank the workers. Plus, the wine isn't yours!"

"I work there, don't I?"

Barnaby was pointing his finger. "Stealing from the vineyard isn't working."

Clarence threw his hands up, utterly defeated. Carissa intervened by stepping between them. She put a hand on both of their shoulders.

"He's here now and he's agreed to join the committee, so that's something, right?"

"Committee? What committee?" Clancy turned sharply to Barnaby.

Barnaby shifted his gaze, along with his feet, and pushed his cousin farther into the restaurant. "Uh, ah, yes, I think I see our table over there. Let's go in. Sooner we order, sooner we eat, right?" He babbled in a blatant attempt to distract Clancy from the fact that he'd been brought there under false pretenses.

Carissa's disapproval turned to an amused grin as she took a step forward to follow. The man next to her bumped her shoulder as he brushed past, causing her to stumble to the side. Thinking at first that she had been standing in the way of an incoming crowd, Carissa stepped even farther to her left, but looking behind her, only a couple people were standing outside the door talking, and none who'd come in. Carissa looked at the man, who'd stopped two paces in front of her and was staring at the restaurant as if he'd never seen a pub before. She moved forward to get a closer look.

With his brown hair, thick-rimmed glasses, the ridiculously large camera strapped around his neck, a backpack on his shoulders, and a book and papers gripped in one hand, he was unmistakably the tourist Cari had seen earlier in the forest. She stepped aside and squinted, trying to remember his name. *What was it? Ron? Richard? Reginald!*

Reginald didn't bother to apologize after walking right into her and seemingly hadn't even noticed. He lifted his camera and took a snapshot of Barnaby and Clarence, now greeting the people at the large table in the middle of the pub. Carissa's eyes flared, and she straightened. The tips of her pointed ears tingled as they caught his words.

"Incredible," the man whispered, "leprechaun or clurichaun?" Reginald put the camera down and opened his book, sifting through the papers stuffed inside. Was he consulting the pages for information on the fae?

Cari's mouth dropped open. No tourist generally knew what the fae were, much less recognized the exact type when they saw them. This one recognized not only her but Barnaby and Clancy, as well. She tensed, her fingers curling into fists. She didn't want to make too much of things, but he had just taken a picture of her friends without them noticing. That warranted a confrontation, didn't it? She took a step forward but stopped when she heard another man call over from his table.

"I'm fairly sure they'd be offended by those labels and even more by your taking pictures of them without their consent." A dapper gentleman with black hair and green eyes sat at a table, the Moss Hill paper sprawled out in front of him. He held his tie back as he leaned forward to lift his drink, then leaned back and said in the most casual tone in which a reprimand had ever been given, "Tell me, do you treat all people of that height like that where you're from? Where I'm from, it's considered rude."

Carissa's cheeks flushed, both because she'd never seen anyone handle a confrontation with such poise and because she realized her eavesdropping was a little rude in itself. She brushed a strand of hair back in place, then walked much slower than necessary toward the table where the decoration committee was seated. She kept the men in her periphery as long as she could without being obvious.

The tourist closed his book with a snap and walked over, some sense of purpose pushing him toward the gentleman. "Those aren't little people." He pointed to Barn and Clancy, speaking quickly and without breath while launching into an explanation of leprechauns.

"Cari, over here." Cameron stood and waved from the table, probably wondering what was taking her so long.

The last she heard was the debonair gentleman inviting Reginald to his table to entertain his stories of fae people. He didn't seem to be mocking the man, which might have been easy to do, but Carissa doubted he'd take the man seriously. At least, Cari hoped he wouldn't. The last thing Moss Hill needed was a bunch of tourists trying to uncover the island's otherworldly secrets.

Carissa half-smiled to Cam and quickened her pace. Cameron sat at the head of the table. Tilly Brier sat on Cameron's right, handing the breadsticks down the table. Across from her, Sheridan Riley, Moss Hill's renowned artist, placed his order with the waitress Cam had called. Darren Ames, and Tim and Patsy Harbridge, all members of the local business association, as well as Cari's neighbor, Rosaleen Alcott, made small talk on opposite sides of the table. Barnaby and Clarence had already taken their seats and seemed to be arguing over the menu.

Cam left his seat, looking behind Carissa and waving. She turned to see Maren and, unsurprisingly, a handful of Maren's friends from all over town.

"Looks like we'll need to add another table." Cam walked past her, calling the attention of another waitress. Carissa greeted Maren in the meantime.

"Glad you showed," Cari teased.

"Of course. I wouldn't have missed it, especially since Cam's paying, right?"

Cam's selective hearing caught that, even from two tables away. "We're all paying our own...unless you're volunteering?" he goaded back.

Maren gave a hearty chuckle. Cari should have laughed too, but couldn't seem to make her smile genuine. Whatever nagging feeling she'd woken up with hadn't left her all day.

"I found a few more helpers." Maren looked pleased with herself, grinning and walking straight to the table. She was oblivious to the men she passed on her right, taking her purse off her shoulder and looking for a seat, which Cam was still working on getting. She introduced Carissa to her friends, Parker and Addison. Her sister, Hattie, Carissa already knew.

Carissa said hello to Hattie and shook hands with Parker. She recalled that the thin, blond man was a relative of Mr. Greer, the town's head librarian. According to Maren, he made a lousy date but a good friend. Addison, tall, tanned and athletic, looked vaguely familiar. He must have been an old classmate based on how Cameron greeted him with a bear hug. Before Cari had a chance to meet him, Cameron pulled him away to help add an extra table to their group.

"I'm not ordering you a drink." Barnaby yanked the menu away from Clarence.

"It's the only thing good on this menu." Clancy attempted to yank it back, nearly knocking over the water glass beside him.

"Whoa," Maren held the glass still and sat down next to Clarence, "looks like I'd better sit here and keep the two of you in line."

"Well, hello." Clancy changed his tune from annoyance to intrigue. He left the menu entirely to Barnaby and shifted his body toward Maren. Carissa couldn't see Maren's face but imagined the mix of skepticism in her eyes.

"Leave her alone." Barnaby smacked Clancy with the menu, and the two were at it again.

Carissa took her seat at the edge of the table, all the way across from Cameron. She couldn't help but notice Tilly scoot her chair just the teensiest bit closer to Cam as he retook his seat. She seemed too comfortable with him.

Too comfortable? Carissa blinked herself out of the thought. There was absolutely no reason why Tilly shouldn't be comfortable with Cameron. They were friends. It wasn't like she was all over him. Though Tilly's honey-colored eyes did seem to brighten as she talked with him.

"Here." Maren handed her a menu. Carissa took it and concentrated on ordering with more attention than she'd ever given the task before. The waitress was two people away anyway, so she needed to decide soon.

"...All the indications that Moss Hill, if that's really what it's called, isn't what it seems to be." She overheard someone speaking from another table. She turned to see Reginald hunched forward, speaking passionately. The added table section had brought her close enough to the two gentlemen to hear what they were saying, though with her elf-ears she probably could have heard them even from the other side of the restaurant. This closely, she almost had to try harder not to hear them.

She turned back to the menu. Her eyes scanned the section headings and entrées, but nothing registered. Maren pondered loudly between the seafood chowder and a potato leek stew.

"Both are good," Carissa said, but the response was automatic. Her mind was on the men's conversation.

"...Rumored to be covered in mist every seven days so that it's not visible to outsiders. This island follows that pattern." The tourist stressed the words.

A smooth voice followed, which had to be the man in the suit. "Too much fog? That's your proof?"

The waitress stood over her, notepad in hand. The mousy brown-haired girl in the red shirt and apron looked straight at Cari. "What can I get you?"

Carissa said the first thing that came to mind—a pasta dish that she had ordered many times before. Her elfish ear twitched the moment the waitress moved on.

She tried not to eavesdrop but couldn't help it. Both her Mossie and fae natures worked against her in this particular case. She tilted her head slightly, listening.

Reg was talking again. "...Local blog, *Musing* something, it actually talked about 'the people of Vale.' But this is Moss Hill, so what's Vale? There's no reference to it anywhere. Unless it's a different kind of 'veil' entirely."

"So," Cameron gathered the attention of the table as the waitress ripped the order sheet off her pad and walked away.

The celebratory committee quieted down. This included Barn and Clancy, who no longer had menus to fight with. "Let's start with setting some dates. I was hoping we could go out to the property tomorrow and get a look at the renovation. It's been going well. A lot has been improved, but the east side is still more ruins than castle."

"That's perfect," Mrs. Harbridge said.

"Yes," Mrs. Alcott added, "thematic for an All Hallows' Eve celebration."

Carissa tried to listen, catching snippets of both her group's conversation and that of the table she was spying on. From them, she heard the gentleman speaking.

"A legendary city with a pub? Amusing."

"No." Reginald seemed undeterred by the sarcastic response. He lowered his voice, making it harder for her to hear. If she'd had human ears, she might not have heard him at all. "I think this town is only a cover."

The man with the silky voice spoke louder. "So, why would it be registered as a county? It's not hidden by any means. I should know, I've got a property under contract here."

"...Nominate Mrs. Harbridge." Mrs. Alcott's voice piped up over the table so that Cari's mind turned back to the discussion at hand.

"Rose, you're very kind." Mrs. Harbridge's face turned red. "But you know Tim's running for president of Moss Hill's business association, and I have the community garden planning this month." It wasn't difficult to discern that the redness of her cheeks was more of a burning anger than a blush.

"Right, I forgot." Mrs. Alcott's crooked smile couldn't have been any faker if she'd worn a cardboard sign that read *insert pretend smile here*. It wasn't complete without the matching backhanded compliment. "The garden really is where you shine. In that case, though—"

"I nominate Carissa to be in charge of decorations," an overzealous Maren chimed in. It was almost worth it to see

Mrs. Alcott thrown for a loop. The older woman's mouth hung open. It was a taste of her own medicine, being interrupted like that, but Cari wished Maren hadn't done it.

Both of Carissa's hands went out in front of her, defensively. "Oh, no, no, no." She tried to disagree, but her throat was dry all of a sudden. Was her face turning red? She might not have been so flustered if she hadn't been caught off guard.

She cleared her throat and tried again. "I have a lot on my plate with apothecary shop." She continued in a ramble longer than she would have liked. If only Cam would stop with his *gotcha* grin she'd be able to speak properly. She might even be able to stop talking. "I'm just not great with art or designs." The words art and design signaled a lightbulb moment, and Cari looked at the artist among them. "Mr. Riley, you could do it." She met Sheridan's dismissive expression with as much hope as she could muster.

Sheridan took a sip of his drink before answering. Carissa didn't miss the scowl Clancy had for Barnaby upon seeing the artist drink. Having had the dramatic pause he most likely had intended, Sheridan looked at Cari like she was missing the point. "My creativity doesn't extend to management. Believe me, I've tried. I'd just be frustrated, and you'd want to get rid of me by the end of it."

"Cari's just modest. She planned the inside layout of the Seelie Tree Apothecary, and she designs all the flyers for the shop. She'll do a great job," Maren said to the table. Turning to Carissa with the same grin as Cameron's, she added, "And besides, if you need ideas, Sheridan just said he'd help." Carissa opened her mouth in disbelief and looked back and forth between Cam and Maren. Those two co-conspirators were guilty by their own self-pleased smiles of backing her into this corner. Thankfully, there were others at the table vain enough to contend with her nomination.

"Cari plainly would rather not," Mrs. Harbridge said. "Oh, excuse me, I don't mean to speak for you, Carissa, but it seems like you'd rather not take on all the fuss of the décor planning.

I know I have a lot to do this month, but since I do have some experience—" Mrs. Harbridge rambled on.

Carissa seemed to be in the clear when Tilly jumped in and voted in Patsy Harbridge's favor. Mr. Ames and Mr. Harbridge agreed. Mrs. Alcott seemed only upset that no one had nominated her. Barnaby supported just about everyone. Clancy agreed with whatever Maren was saying. Maren's friends seemed not to care one way or the other.

Cameron made the executive decision to move on to other aspects of the festival. The food arrived, and the conversation flowed more naturally, turning to what activities they'd offer and how they would do fundraising both before and during the event. Carissa tried to follow along, making suggestions when and where she could, but her mind kept getting drawn back to the other table. She felt compelled to continue her eavesdropping, trying to listen enough to her own table not to arouse suspicion. She felt like a criminal, but her attention jumped between discussions almost against her will.

Reginald defined fae folk almost as well as a Mossie could. Cameron talked about a dinner he was attending with the mayor that could help increase funds for the celebration. The gentleman argued with the tourist, saying that he knew the mayor personally and had never heard him refer to any fae. Mr. Harbridge talked about offering discounts from local businesses as prizes. Reginald argued that several Mossies in this very pub were not what they appeared to be. Barnaby asked whether he should spread the word that they would be inviting the people of Vale. Reg said he knew a man who could prove to him the existence of Hy Brasil—home of the faerie people.

Carissa dropped her fork.

Only Maren seemed to notice the look on Carissa's face, which must have been pale and then red as the blood rushed from her ears to her cheeks. She asked if anything was wrong. Carissa had enough awareness to say no.

Maren waved down a waiter for another utensil. It didn't matter. With a sick feeling growing in her stomach, Cari wasn't hungry anyway. When she couldn't hear the two men speaking anymore, her heart pounded in her ears. Had they heard Barnaby's comment about Vale? Had her dropping the fork made them realize she'd been listening? And why was this tourist talking to the gentleman anyway? They seemed like they'd just met, or did they know each other? If the gentleman was a resident of Moss Hill, Carissa had never seen him before.

Cari bent to her side and reached for her fork, trying to see what she could hear at the other table. The pause in the men's conversation was brief. The excited tourist continued right as the metal touched Carissa's fingertips.

"There's something strange about this place, I'm telling you. Even if this ends up not being Hy Brasil, trust me, this is not a normal town."

The blood was pumping in her ears as she resumed an upright position. She didn't realize that all eyes were on her. That did nothing to relieve her mind, but she resumed a relaxed face and smiled as if nothing was bothering her.

"So, what do you think, Carissa?" Cameron asked. He was serious now, not holding that silly grin on his face but leaning on the table with both elbows, as if eager for a response.

She looked to Maren for a clue, but only got the wide-eyed, enthusiastic smile that Maren often wore when she wanted Carissa to agree with her. The problem was, she didn't know what she would be agreeing on, or to, for that matter.

Carissa swallowed and tried for a neutral answer. "I'm with the committee, whatever you all decide."

The minute Cameron's smile broadened like the Cheshire Cat, she knew she was in trouble. "Great, well, that settles it. I'll take care of fundraising and overall arrangement. Mrs. Harbridge and Mrs. Alcott will split the activities planning, and Carissa will organize decorations. I think we should meet at Fairfield tomorrow at 9:00 a.m. for a quick look at the castle grounds. I think we're off to a good start."

Carissa opened her mouth to object. The Seelie Tree Apothecary was open on Saturdays. How could she lead a subcommittee if she couldn't make the first meeting?

"Don't worry," Maren leaned toward Carissa, whispering, "I can cover the morning shift."

Carissa felt the heat growing over her face, especially after the group all rose to leave. She probably should have been listening, but she blamed Maren and Cam for setting her up like this.

Turning, she caught a glimpse of Reginald as she reached for her purse. They locked eyes a moment, and something in his face told her he'd definitely taken an interest in her group, whether it was because he recognized Cari or because he heard the word "Vale" at least once from the group.

"A good start," Cameron had said. Carissa watched the tourist gather his things and walk out of the pub door. A good start, or the beginning of trouble for Moss Hill?

Chapter 4

Scaredy Sprite

As soon as Reginald left the pub, another gentleman with a familiar face entered. Edris Everly, the business tycoon, passed right by Carissa without seeming to notice she was there. She stepped out of the entryway by the cashier's register and traced his path with her eyes. A waitress came over to him, but Carissa was distracted by her party walking past her.

"See you tomorrow, Cari." Maren walked out hand in hand with Parker. That wasn't a good sign after all the reasons she'd listed why she'd never go out with him again. Carissa gave a tight-lipped smile, partly because of her friend's bad decision making in getting close to Parker again, and partly to show she was still annoyed with her friend for volunteering her for the subcommittee leader. Maren's giggling could be heard even past the glass door. She'd deal with her later.

Addison walked silently behind them, and Hattie passed with a "say hi to your nan for me."

Carissa nodded in return.

"'Night, Cari." Barnaby pushed a surly Clancy out of the pub. The clurichaun grumbled something along the lines of how stupid the whole committee planning meeting had been.

Carissa's smile faded, and she gave a sympathetic look as she said goodnight to Barnaby.

Mr. Ames, Mr. and Mrs. Harbridge, and Mrs. Alcott left in a hubbub of conversation, yet Mrs. Alcott still took the time to pass a look back and forth between Carissa and Cameron. Cari clenched her teeth and gripped her purse tighter, knowing that the old gossip was formulating her own theories about whom Cari was waiting for and how Cam's lagging behind with Tilly and Sheridan might be causing her jealousy. Well, she wasn't waiting for Cam. And she wasn't jealous.

She had nothing to be jealous of. Who cared if the party had left and the three of them were standing around the empty table talking? What did it matter that Cam seemed highly interested in whatever Tilly was saying, or that she gently patted his arm as she looked across him to Sheridan? They could be talking about anything.

And Cam isn't mine to worry about anyway.

She wondered why she had to add that as an afterthought. Her gaze had already lingered too long on them. She turned her attention to where it should've been in the first place. Or rather, where it shouldn't have been, since Mr. Everly's business was not her own. She wasn't sure why she felt the need to stay and see with whom he was meeting.

The middle-aged gentleman, who'd been the voice of reason in the conversation with the tourist, folded his paper as soon as Mr. Everly was in his line of sight. He stood, flattening his blue tie against his dark suit and extending a hand to greet the businessman. Something in Cari's gut told her that this was unsurprising. It was almost the most logical circumstance she could have expected.

"Sorry that I'm late. Were you waiting long?" Carissa had never seen Mr. Everly up close before. She hadn't realized how much he sounded like Alden. Since Alden was his son, it was probably the other way around. The dark hair and tall height had been inherited, too. But his face was longer and thinner than Alden's, and he carried himself with hubris where

Alden showed hesitation. His tone spoke less of an apology than an inconvenience to himself. The pressure this father must've put on his son.... Carissa flinched just imagining it.

"Yes." The gentleman always sounded half-amused while speaking, Cari noticed. "But by choice," he continued. "I like to arrive ahead of schedule. Gives me time to take in the local culture."

Mr. Everly looked at his phone, putting one hand in his pocket nonchalantly. "Fudge," he looked up and smiled, clarifying, "my butler, has the car outside waiting to take us to the estate if you're ready."

The man gestured to the door. "Lead on." His blue eyes rested on Cari. She abruptly looked away. She was standing there, purse in hand, watching a pair of strangers. Could she be more obvious? Was his glancing at her purely coincidence, or had he known she was eavesdropping the whole time?

She dared not look at the two men again. Her eyes naturally drifted back to Cam, another mistake. She caught his gaze when he looked away from Tilly. Now it would look like she was staring at him. To cover her mistake, she nodded and smiled, waving at him as if she was just saying goodbye.

She turned right in front of the two businessmen and jetted out of the pub just before they did. The door seemed to open automatically and held itself in place. Carissa twisted to look at it as she stepped onto the pavement outside. She saw the hand, bearing an expensive silver watch with a large face, and turned to thank the man behind her who'd held the door open.

The gentleman politely waved off Cari's thanks. "Don't mention it." His smile was caring, radiating from his eyes more than his lips. He was about Alden's father's age, but there was something older, more grandfatherly about his expression.

Mr. Everly followed behind, preoccupied with something on his phone. The man continued holding the door for him, and Mr. Everly uttered a meaningless "thanks" as he walked through it.

Carissa continued on her way a few feet in front of the gentlemen.

"Mr. Everly!" she heard Tilly's voice ring out behind her.

Carissa turned to catch a glimpse of Tilly and Cam walking over to the two. Cameron just happened to look up at precisely the wrong time. That was twice now that he'd seen her watching him. Carissa busied herself by looking for her keys in her purse. What they had to talk about, Cari couldn't begin to guess, but she didn't want to stick around for any more awkward exchanges. She continued digging through her bright green purse while making her way to the car Nan had let her borrow.

"Cari, wait a moment," Cam's voice followed her.

He jogged over, standing beside her just Carissa's hand settled on the keys. She stopped and turned around, keychain in hand.

"I forgot to ask you to dinner."

Cari held back a smile and waited for him to realize he hadn't made sense, considering they'd just left from dinner. Holding back the smile was more difficult than she'd thought.

"Not this dinner, obviously. I mean I forgot to mention the dinner at the Everly's. They're holding a welcome dinner for Mr. MacLir." He looked back at the group behind them.

So that's Mr. MacLir? Though it didn't erase the strangeness of his conversation with the tourist, at least she understood who the gentleman was and his association with the Everlys. The wealthiest people in town would, of course, befriend the man whose company was investing in the town's future.

Cam continued, "And it's doubling as a fundraising event all in one. They invited the committee leaders and seeing as you are one now...."

"I understand," Cari took her cue. "What time should I be there?" She knew he was trying to ask her if she'd go with him, but she so enjoyed the flustered redness of his face.

"Would you like to go together?" he asked properly.

"If you want." She shrugged, but her smile said it all.

He was positively exuberant when he turned around and rejoined the group. Carissa might have had a little extra pep in her step as well as she made her way down the narrow streets. By the time she reached the car, however, her mind had drifted back to the conversation on Hy Brasil. She thought back on everything and didn't catch up with her surroundings until she was nearly home.

When she pulled up to the driveway, she was greeted with a certain little nature faerie sitting on the rose bushes in the front yard. Carissa navigated into the garage. She hated driving, even more so when she had to steer it precisely between shelving and storage boxes. At least Nan's car was a small hybrid. Once the car was parked, Carissa walked back out to greet the sprite.

"Chaos? What are you doing out here?"

Chaos, sitting cross-legged and cross-armed, placed both hands flat on the rose she was sitting on and pushed herself up, right to the tip of Cari's nose. The tiny tan fairy with the red wings, in her signature purple frock, looked Carissa dead in the eye with serious determination. She clapped Cari on the nose and pulled her toward the door.

"Ow!" Carissa swatted at the faerie, gently but firmly reprimanding her. "What on earth?" She rubbed her nose and took a defensive step back.

Chaos made a full circle with her arm as she floated to the door as if saying, *follow me.* The force with which she jabbed her index finger toward the door added a sense of urgency. The sprite's reddening face told Cari that she was angry.

"Are you fighting with Hiya and Cynth again?"

Chaos folded her arms and turned her head to the side in a huff.

"No." Carissa let go of her injury and walked back to the garage. "I'm not getting involved in another one of your arguments with them."

She could hear Chaos chiming behind her with the bell-like sound that sprites made when they flustered with emotion. It was the only sound they were capable of and a beautiful faint cadence often mistaken for the wind. It had a less pleasing discordance when the emotion being expressed was anger.

Cari ignored the sound and passed into the house, clicking the button to shut the garage behind her. Chaos zoomed into the kitchen and pointed furiously at the window over the sink. She signed like crazy but was going far too fast for Cari to understand. Cari had gotten better at comprehending Chaos, though she still struggled compared to how effortlessly she communicated with the nature faeries she'd grown up with, like Hiya and Cynth. Right now, she didn't even want to try.

Nan came into the kitchen and opened the fridge, taking out the leftover Bundt cake she'd baked for the last poetry club meeting. Without even greeting Carissa, she explained warily about Chaos's latest grievance against the troublesome duo.

"They're teasing her because her wings are turning black. She's sensitive about it." Nan took out two plates and opened the drawer, retrieving two forks. "Want a slice?"

Carissa couldn't believe Nan was acting so casual about this. "What? Chaos, let me see."

She dashed over to Chaos and pulled the sprite into her palm. Cari examined the wings. The tips were, in fact, darker. Chaos wriggled in her grasp and slapped her hands away. The nature faerie rolled her eyes and pointed out the window. The chocolate cosmos plant she was attached to was sitting in a basket by the side of the house. The little plant had grown heartily but was barely visible from the window, even when Carissa gripped the counter, leaned over the sink, and stretched her head out past the glass.

"What, what is it? Is the plant okay?"

Nan answered, "The new root you planted is growing." Carissa pulled herself back into the kitchen. Nan was cutting the second slice and setting it onto the next empty plate. "She showed it to me today."

Carissa peered over the sink and out the window again. Chocolate cosmos' seeds were not fertile. They required cutting and replanting of a new root to grow fresh flowers.

Since the sprite was linked in spirit with the plant, changes in one might naturally affect the other. Seeing the plant, she breathed out a relieved sigh.

"Oh, Chaos, that's all right," Cari said. "The new flowers are just coming in darker than the last ones. Your connection to the plant is making your wings darker, too."

Chaos folded her arms and tilted her head, looking at Carissa from the top of her eyeline. She thrust her arm toward the window and ranted again. Apparently, Nan could understand the nature faerie now.

"She knows. She wants you to tell that to Hiya and Cynth," Nan said. "They're being quite pixieish about it." Setting the plates on the round kitchen table by the sliding doors, Nan called to Chaos to join them. Usually, Chaos would have zoomed toward sweets, but this time she glided slowly and daintily over, keeping her head up and her eyes fixed in front, ignoring Cari. It was her way of showing that she was still upset with Carissa for not taking her seriously. Cari had come to learn that sassiness was one of Chaos's many eccentricities.

"I'll talk to them," Carissa sulked, following the sprite and Nan to a seat.

Chaos made no response.

"I promise," Cari stressed.

Chaos still wouldn't look at her. Carissa realized the minuscule, proud faerie was waiting for an apology.

"I'm sorry I was dismissive of you," Carissa obliged. This warranted a long glance from Chaos. The sprite kept her eyes on Cari with a placid expression on her face while she tucked a long napkin in the collar of her dress. The eyes stayed locked on her while the sprite grabbed a handful of cake and put it in her mouth. Finally, Chaos closed her eyes and gave a curt nod, accepting Cari's apology.

Carissa let out a breath, glad the sprite had finally come to her senses. She took a full heap of the Bundt cake herself. Chai spiced—it was delicious. Cari's stomach growled as if the taste reminded her she was hungry. She really hadn't eaten much at the restaurant.

"Mmm, Nan, you outdid yourself. I think this might be your best cake yet." Carissa closed her eyes for a moment, savoring the moist, airy goodness.

"Thank you," Nan said. "Chaos helped."

Carissa opened her eyes and grinned at the nature faerie. "Really? You've got a real knack for it. Well done." Carissa tipped her fork in appreciation before taking her next bite.

Chaos beamed. The smile was far better than her previous anger. But Nan wasn't smiling, Cari kicked herself for not noticing earlier.

"Is something bothering you, Nan?"

Nan looked up from her cake. Her knitted brow displayed confusion.

"No." She laughed. "I can see why you think that. No, not at all, just thinking about the library. Mr. Greer has asked me to work more hours since one of the part-time assistants quit. I suppose I have nothing else to do, so I might as well." Nan put down her fork, breathed deep, and swallowed. Then, she looked up. "Seems like something is bothering you, though."

Carissa realized she was motionless with a forkful in her hands and a grave look on her face, slumping her shoulders. She straightened and put down her fork. "There is." She explained about the conversation she overheard, down to the last detail she could remember.

Taking her napkin, Nan wiped her mouth and set it back down on the table. "You can't draw conclusions yet. It could just be one lone conspiracy theorist," Nan chortled. "Or a future Mossie, who knows?" She pushed her finished plate away. "I would talk to Tilly, though, if I were you."

Carissa froze. "Tilly?" Her voice pitched itself higher than she intended. She hadn't said a word to Nan about Tilly or Cameron. How could she have known? For that matter, what was it exactly that there was for her to know?

"*Mossie Musings.* That's Tilly's blog," Nan clarified.

Carissa leaned forward and put a hand to her head, laughing silently at herself. Of course. She'd seen it just this morning.

"She just quit the library," Nan said, referring to the assistant who had quit. "Apparently, her freelance work has picked up. She's even written for the newspaper now and again. Between the blog, her theater work, and her writing, she's been quite busy."

Busy making moves on Cameron, too, it seemed. Carissa shook the thought out of her head. She had no idea what such a notion was doing there in the first place or why it kept coming back.

Cari picked up her plate and Nan's. Chaos was still devouring the piece Nan had set on a napkin for her.

"I was also made the leader of the decorations subcommittee."

"Congratulations."

"Ugh. I'm not really looking forward to it. I've never led a project like this." Carissa turned on the water to wash up the dishes in the sink.

"What are you talking about? You and the nature faeries decorated the whole school garden for that performance of *Elves and the Seasons.*"

Carissa placed the second plate on the drying rack and wiped her hands on the towel draped over the cabinet under the sink. She turned around, confused. *"Elves and the Seasons?* Nan, that was primary school. And the nature faeries did all the work. All they did was make the flowers bloom. And all I did was encourage them."

"That's what I call leadership," Nan said, the proud parental smile lighting her face.

Carissa let out a stifled laugh, not sure whether Nan was serious or just teasing. Probably both. She was perhaps trying to ease her discomfort at having been chosen to lead, but it wasn't working.

Chaos, who had perked up upon hearing Carissa and Nan's mention of the nature faeries, nodded in agreement with Nan.

"So, what is it they want you to decorate?" Nan asked, resting an elbow on the table and cupping her chin.

Chaos pulled the napkin off her neck and wiped her whole face, then flew over to where Carissa was leaning back against the counter. She sat on her shoulder while Cari explained.

"They want to turn Fairfield Castle into a haunted house for a town-wide celebration, Vale included." Carissa gave a few details about the project, the little she had paid attention to at the dinner.

"Sounds interesting," Nan said.

"Sounds like a lot of work," Cari retorted.

"Well then, you'd better get started." Nan stood up, gathering Chaos's discarded napkin to throw in the trash. "You want some help?"

Carissa shrugged, forgetting that a nature faerie was resting on her. She looked at disgruntled Chaos while she said, "No, I think I'll just look at some inspiration pictures, brainstorm a little tonight."

Carissa said goodnight to Nan and to Chaos, but unlike Nan who'd gone into the sitting room for some evening reading, Chaos refused to go back to the garden.

"You want me to talk to Hiya and Cynth right now?" Carissa attempted to get Chaos off her shoulder, but the sprite wouldn't hop into her open hand.

The nature faerie pointed to the hall where the stairs led up to Cari's bedroom. Now Carissa understood. "You heard us talk about the nature faeries helping with the play and now you want to help with the castle?"

Chaos gave an exaggerated nod and lifted herself up to pat Cari's head as if she were an obedient pet.

Cari was too mentally exhausted to argue, so she just complied with her boss—at least, it was quickly becoming clear that Chaos was the boss in this relationship. Carissa trudged upstairs with the sprite on her shoulder.

She took a seat on her bed with her tablet, sifting through pictures with Chaos of haunted houses and city-wide celebrations of All Hallows' Eve in various counties and countries. Some of them were intricate. Chaos recognized the images of Día de los Muertos, the Day of the Dead, from her hometown in Mexico. She pointed and danced on top of the screen. She jumped up, startled, and hovered over the tablet when it moved to the next screen at the touch of her foot. Once she realized that it was her who had changed the picture, she flicked the screen again to scroll to the next image. The tablet was now wholly in her hands.

Having lost control of the device, Carissa walked across the room to her desk and opened her laptop. It glowed to life. Her hands hesitated on the keyboard. It wasn't decorations she had on her mind. She brought up the browser and typed into the search engine the name of Tilly's blog.

Mossie Musings came up with a new post, marked just twenty minutes ago. Nan was right. Tilly certainly had been keeping herself busy. The title of the post read: "Magnus MacLir, leader of MacLir Properties, to Attend Everly Estate Dinner."

According to the post, Mr. MacLir had arrived earlier that day and met with a few locals at the Second Street Pub. There was no mention of Reginald Smith specifically, and no indication that she'd overheard their conversation. Cari's eyes skimmed over the whole article, taking in the gist. She stopped when she came to the mention of Cameron Larke, the mayor's official liaison to the people of Vale.

Didn't Tilly realize how risky it was to keep mentioning Vale in an online publication? Carissa read the quote attributed to Cam. He'd apparently said that MacLir's foresight was "exactly what Moss Hill needed" and that he would be "a welcome change to the island."

Carissa pursed her lips. She wasn't sure she agreed with Cam anymore on whether the renovation projects and advertising campaigns were good for Moss Hill. Especially given what she'd overheard tonight, she was becoming more and more convinced that the changes were not beneficial. Was that the feeling of dread that had been following her around all day?

She skimmed over several articles from the past few days. One, in particular, seemed important: "Eamon O'Brien Returns to Moss Hill." She clicked the post.

"Eamon O'Brien, the grandson of the late Mayor George O'Brien and owner of the Moss Hill Marina and Fishing Company, returned to Moss Hill Thursday morning. Long presumed dead in a boating accident, O'Brien said only that he was prevented by circumstance from returning to Moss Hill these last five years. His wife, Mary O'Brien, said that it was a 'miracle' and that she is glad to have him back alive. When asked what his plans were now that he's returned, O'Brien said that he plans 'to claim what is rightfully his and restore the O'Briens to their proper standing in Moss Hill.' What he means by this is unclear but will perhaps be revealed in due time."

Carissa remembered O'Brien. She hadn't seen him since she went off to college, but his wife was a regular customer and a good friend of Nan's. She smiled to herself. This was good news, even if O'Brien seemed a little cryptic in Tilly's interview. Carissa moved the mouse to close down the internet window. Something in her stopped the action.

Carissa's fingers hovered over the keyboard. There was one more thing she had to look up before she could get a peaceful night's rest. Slowly, she typed in the words that she hadn't been able to get out of her mind since she'd overheard it at the pub.

The cursor blinked at her, daring her to press enter. She stared at the screen where the words *Hy Brasil* were written in the search bar.

Enter.

"Hy Brasil: a mysterious island west of the UK, said to be covered in mist and hidden from human eyes, is the home of supernatural people often linked to faerie mythology.

"The island was said to have been visited rarely by ships, but the encounters occurred often enough throughout history to have been included in ancient maps. Encounters show that the beings living on the island had powers far beyond mortals' comprehension."

Carissa read on. The stories and legends of a land where the faeries hid away from humans sounded enough like Moss Hill, but with descriptions that were far more magical than anything their little town had to offer. The internet was full of fanciful stories. It was only a matter of convincing tourists that Moss Hill didn't belong in any of the tales. She looked at the faerie happily tapping away at the tablet on her bed. She had no idea how they were going to manage that.

Chapter 5

Spooky Specters

It was cold on the castle grounds at 9:00 a.m. Carissa's long-sleeved, light purple sweater did little to stop the chill that shivered down her spine. Her purse, secured across her body, shielded her a little from the wind. Her frizzled hair whipped in her face while she set her bicycle against the granite outer wall surrounding the castle and used her elf-magic to sink it slightly into the ground. It was unfathomable that anyone would try to steal it, especially in a remote meeting like this with only the committee members attending, but she'd formed the habit of using her magic in place of a bicycle lock. Not using it would have felt odd.

Odd feelings were becoming normal for her these days. She shuddered from more than just the wind as she wandered through the ruins. It was never a good idea to arrive first to a supposedly haunted castle. Ever since part of one wall fell in while sidhe guards had been there searching for a leanansidhe who'd been causing trouble, people talked about how the renovation work had disturbed a spirit.

Ghosts, spirits of the dead, apparitions, they were all as frightening to the fae as they were to humans. The

Otherworld of the fae was not the same as the world beyond, and neither human nor faerie had ventured there to know much about it at all. Ghosts were not common in Moss Hill. Carissa could think of only one that she and Cameron knew and even that, according to Cam, was too many.

Carissa suspected Cam had been happy to see his old school friend returned to, well, not to life, but to Moss Hill at least. In his ankou form, Alden Everly's skeletal specter was fearsome to behold, but he had the power to change to his human form, which allowed Cam to feel better around him. Cari was grateful to the ankou for saving her life in the past.

Why she was thinking of him now, Carissa blamed on the eeriness of the old castle. From the outside, the fortress appeared to have been rebuilt strongly enough. The stones carried the weight of the message intended by the original builders: *Keep out, unless invited.* Towers on either end of the massive wall protruded from the ground like swords.

The spookiness only increased as she passed the large opening of the gatehouse. It loomed over her so that she wondered if an iron gate would come crashing down as she entered the castle's outer walls. But no, the old iron had been removed before the renovation and replaced with a newly secured wood lattice. It was open now, leading Cari to think someone was here already.

The stone walls—ramparts, as they were called—protected the entire castle. They had been redone masterfully. Massive wooden buttresses added sturdy support. The cold, grey structure guarded an open courtyard, which Carissa gasped upon seeing.

Newly set slate tiles glistened with the dew of morning, surrounding three circular areas meant for grass, which hadn't been planted as yet. A massive tower to the right, called a *keep*, attached to the side wall and used for defense in case of invasion, was still undone. She walked closer to it.

It must have been a splendid sight to behold in its past days of glory. But now it was weathered and worn. The window at the top, where soldiers might have once stood guard, was empty and dark. The glory, for good or ill, was gone.

Carissa slowly made her way to the castle itself. It stretched all the way across the courtyard on the opposite end of the gate. Massive as it was, it, too, had only been partly redone. The great hall in the center and the right side of the castle, nearest the keep, looked brand-new, at least from the outside. She'd never seen it like this before, with the stones practically shining in the humid air.

She dared not go inside—not alone. Instead, she walked around the left side of it, as if compelled to see the ruins. The section she was looking at was still unfinished; construction had been halted. The rubble showing through crumbling walls was visible without getting too close. The entire west wing was left unfinished, as was the keep on the east front corner.

Carissa made her way back to the center of the courtyard, picturing the décor. She could put giant welcome banners above the gate, a dark one with some clichéd message like *Welcome Boys and Ghouls*; that type of thing was almost a given for any town-wide bash.

Looking above the entryway, her eyes raced to the top of the rampart walls. Based on her knowledge, Cari knew there were walkways atop the entire wall's structure. A few wooden enclosures had been remade in some sections as places of refuge during battle.

The top of the wall raised and lowered like the classic rook chess piece. These were once used as places for archers to aim at intruders. For the celebrations, they'd be the perfect area to decorate. Candles would look nice in the square hallows between the...what were they called? She stood there, trying to recall a grade school report on the castle when a shadow moved in one of the embrasures between the merlons. That's what the hollow sections were called, embrasures, and the raised parts of the wall were the merlons.

The figure was only there a second, then it was gone. She froze. Her mouth hung wide, and her eyes searched the wall. Slowly reacting to the alarm bells in her mind, she turned around, surveying the entire structure. She saw nothing. Whatever it was had left.

Or not.

She clutched her chest and gasped with the sudden appearance of a specter form right beside her.

"Cari?"

Alden's face appeared in front of her, quickly turning fully human. His dark ankou eyes faded to blue. He seemed as surprised as she was, but concern followed as he reached out to steady her.

Carissa didn't bat him away but closed her eyes and opened them again to assure herself it was only the ankou. Her sigh of relief came out as a laugh. There was some irony in being relieved to see the Grim Reaper.

Her hand, still on her heart, slowly fell away and she assured Alden she was all right. "You nearly scared me to death. What are you doing here?"

"I could ask you the same." Alden seemed to realize that his hands had lingered around her arms too long. He pulled away and straightened.

"The decoration committee is turning Fairfield Castle into a haunted house for the All Hallows' Eve celebration." Carissa folded her arms. The cold was returning now that she had calmed down.

Alden's eyes traveled over the castle. "I'm not sure that's a good idea."

Cari followed his gaze. "Why not?"

"Ankous are drawn to places for a reason."

Carissa put a hand to her forehead, pushing back the few strands of red.

"Are you saying you were drawn to Fairfield? Is something going to happen here?"

"I can't say for sure. It doesn't feel like a collecting."

Cari felt her skin crawl at the word *collecting*. Collecting of souls is what he meant.

"I thought I saw the barguest here yesterday morning."

Alden's lack of surprise caused a spine-tingling sensation at the base of her neck.

"I've seen it around town as well. It was at the marina yesterday afternoon," Alden revealed.

The marina seemed like an odd place, but no one had died there, as far as she knew. Carissa took comfort in that, at least.

The sound of cars coming up the gravel road caused Cari to turn and Alden to vanish. She glanced back at the air where Alden stood a moment ago, wondering what, if anything, she should do. Should she say something to the group? Would something awful happen to one of them here this morning? Was the whole town in danger of some impending doom? Or was she just overreacting?

Her legs hastened the moment she gathered enough courage to move. Outside the courtyard, two cars had come up the drive. The first, a black luxury vehicle, belonged to Mr. Everly. Carissa recognized the driver as Fudge, the Everly's butler. He parked and exited the vehicle, circling around the side to open the door for Mr. Everly and his guest, Magnus MacLir. Cameron had also come with them. He reached inside to assist Jane Everly in stepping onto the gravel terrain.

The second car Carissa knew well. Mrs. Alcott and Mrs. Harbridge emerged from the turquoise SUV. The sight of the two arguing over who-knows-what as they tread carefully over the rocky ground in their 1980s attire—a maroon dress in Mrs. Alcott's case and brown pantsuit in Mrs. Harbridge's—eased Cari a bit. It was a very normal exchange and seemingly no villain in sight to cause any more mayhem than the duo could produce themselves.

Though, she didn't know Mr. MacLir well enough to make any assumptions about him yet. She continued forward toward the car. Her attention focused on the man while he was busy taking in the sight of Fairfield. She couldn't imagine the warm smile on his sturdy jawline ever twisting out of malice to a threat. She had been recently fooled by a villain in disguise, but not completely. The hobgoblin in her last brush with death had always seemed a little shady, in foresight. And he'd killed one of Mr. MacLir's employees, too, as she recalled. If anything, MacLir was a victim of dark fae as much as any Mossie who'd encountered them these last few months.

Carissa kept walking right up to the car. Alden's sister, Jane, greeted her with open arms. Carissa wasn't much of a hugging person, but she didn't mind. In the little time that she'd gotten to know Jane, she came to see her as a considerate and sensitive person. They didn't seem to be traits inherited from her parents.

Without so much as a hello to Carissa, Mr. Everly called out, "If you'll come with me, Mr. MacLir, I'll show you the improvements they've already made."

MacLir tipped his head at Carissa. The slight wrinkles around his eyes creased, and his lips pulled into an apologetic smile. Whether he recognized her or not was unclear, but the small gesture was appreciated. She returned it with a smile. Mr. MacLir followed Mr. Everly, leaving the others to congregate outside.

"It's so good to see you." Jane ended the embrace, shifting over to Fudge's arm. She leaned on him as they walked over the stones to the grass just outside the castle. Her tailored, black coat and grey pantsuit made her about the only person in Moss Hill with modern dress sense.

"Good morning, Cari," Cam offered his shoulder. It was too over the top for Carissa, given that they were here to plan an event. She gave a hello to both of them and tugged her mulberry cardigan, wrapping it around herself as she folded her arms.

"I told you it looked like rain. I'm sure I felt a raindrop. I'm going back for my umbrella." Mrs. Alcott put her hand out and clicked the button on her keychain to unlock the car doors.

"It's not raining, and even if it was, a little rain won't kill you. Good morning, Carissa," Mrs. Harbridge said in one breath. She walked so fast she passed Cari and Cam and was ahead of the group and at the castle wall in a few seconds.

There, she leaned against the rampart wall and took off her shoe, releasing a pebble.

Mrs. Alcott kept to her words and walked back to the car. That strange feeling returned. Cari thought about Alden's words. What if a spirit or something attacked while they were separated? What if a wall caved in again or some other tragedy struck while they were there? She opened her mouth to speak, but Jane began before she could.

"Cam's probably already told you about the dinner." Jane let go of Fudge as they stood on the grass by Fairfield's entrance.

Smiling, Jane waved a hand to Fudge, who took out three fancy envelopes with old-fashioned seals and textured words indented on the front. He handed one to Carissa and one to Mrs. Harbridge. The third, Carissa assumed, was for Mrs. Alcott.

Cari's fingers traced her name on the front. The front seal was the symbol of a tree branch with fruit on it. Just a fancy stamp or the Everly family crest? Did the Everlys have a family crest? Cari had no idea.

She waited to open it, as she thought it was polite. Mrs. Alcott took hers and broke the seal immediately. Mrs. Harbridge rolled her eyes, watching.

"Since you're leading the subcommittees for the All Hallows' Eve celebration, and it's being held at the site of Mr. MacLir's largest project on the island, my father agreed that you shouldn't miss the dinner welcoming Mr. MacLir to Moss Hill."

"Excellent," Mrs. Alcott praised.

"Thank you for the invitation," Mrs. Harbridge's tone stressed formality. Mrs. Alcott's head fell just slightly in a huff, showing that the one-upmanship hadn't been lost on her.

Carissa issued her thanks as well, but half-heartedly. A room full of high-browed people wasn't appealing, especially given how much she'd had to deal with the sidhe lately. One couldn't get more high-brow than those self-centered, all-important faeries. A room full of humans, even if they turned out to be as haughty as they were rich, might not be so bad in comparison.

"I know it's short notice," Jane seemed to read her mind, "but we'd love for you to come."

"We wouldn't miss it." Mrs. Harbridge spoke for herself and her husband.

"Ow!" Mrs. Alcott's loud cry reverberated through the cold air. She rubbed the side of her forehead vigorously and scowled at Patsy Harbridge. Her face scrunched in fury. "Patsy, how could you?"

"How could I what?" Mrs. Harbridge asked, genuinely surprised.

"You threw that rock at me."

"The pebble in my shoe? Are you serious?" Mrs. Harbridge waved her off with a flick of her hand.

"How childish!" The woman in maroon stomped toward the group.

Mrs. Harbridge turned sharply on her heels, away from Mrs. Alcott's sneer. "Even my seven-year-old knows not to throw rocks—or accuse people of throwing them. Whatever you felt, it wasn't me." She hadn't even finished her sentence when she walked straight past the entrance to the courtyard and into the castle ruins.

Carissa tried to yell out a warning to stop her, but what would she say? *You can't go in there. My friend, the Grim Reaper, thinks something is wrong here.* That was an utterly mad thing to say. What's worse, being Mossies, they'd probably believe her and call the mayor out for a full investigation. The mention of fae scaring humans would lead to a sidhe investigation, and the sidhe were the only people powerful enough to eradicate an ankou.

She couldn't do that to Alden. She had to get them out of there before someone got hurt, and she had to do it without mentioning why they needed to leave. Why, or when, had life in Moss Hill gotten so complicated?

"This courtyard is perfect!" Mrs. Harbridge admired. "We'll have the ticket booth in the front." She pointed beside the gatehouse between two buttresses.

Mrs. Alcott, who had walked as far from her rival as one possibly could, closer to the great hall, felt the need to speak louder. "Food tables in this area and kids can bob for apples back here."

Jane nodded her agreement, or possibly amusement, and her butler took notes on what the ladies were saying. The two went on like it was a competition for Fudge's attention. Cari's heartbeat increased with their volume. The wind rustled, a random leaf catching Cari's eye as it flew past. She saw no one but had the distinct feeling they were being watched. *It must be Alden.* She tried to console herself. But was that a consolation? And was it even Alden?

Cameron, evidently unaware of any problem, conversed with Jane and Mrs. Harbridge. Carissa followed the movement of his hands as he pointed to the stained-glass windows beside the gatehouse.

"The oriels are the original windows, just touched up," Cam said.

She watched Mrs. Alcott walk closer to the great hall's entrance and tried to get Cam's attention with a look or a wave, but she couldn't wait for him to catch on. Seeing her turn and take an interest in the ruins, Carissa hurried her pace.

This succeeded in drawing Cam's eye, though he had no way of knowing that fear was moving her feet so rapidly. Cameron left Jane admiring the stained glass and practically jogged over to Cari. He called out to the group as he went.

"Great idea, let's take a look at the main hall, through here. Once you see the renovations inside, you'll be astounded by the improvements."

Cari was annoyed by how much Cam was sounding like the mayor, especially when she had such a dire need to stop him from entering the castle. Carissa grabbed Cam's arm as soon as she was close enough. She had little time to convince him to turn them all back as the others meandered over.

"No, Cam," Cari whispered. "We have to get them out of here." Cari's attention shifted between every corner and crevice of the outer walls. From where she stood, she was blocking the entryway into the castle. Cam sidestepped, breaking her grip on him. She held him tighter and parsed her lips to form another argument.

Cam placed a firm hand on hers. "You're nervous about being on the committee, I understand. Maybe Maren and I shouldn't have pushed you into this—"

"Watch out!" Mrs. Alcott shouted. She pointed above their heads. Carissa and the others looked to see grey stone falling from a window right above Mrs. Harbridge's head.

Lucky for Mrs. Harbridge, Fudge was spry for a...how old was he, anyway? He grabbed her arms and pulled her out of the way from a considerable chunk of cement that seemed to have been hurled at her from the top of the keep.

Carissa ran to her side, diverted by Cam, who dashed without hesitation past her and into the large building. Within moments, he was above the rampart walls, running toward the keep. She bit her lip and traced her eyes ahead of him, worried about what might be waiting for him at his destination. This time, she saw the shadow of a person at the top of the keep.

"Cameron!" she yelled out.

The dark shadow lingered long enough for Cari to sense its eyes on her. Though she couldn't clearly see it, she had a strong sense that whatever it was had not just watched the object fall, but had caused it.

A shudder jolted Cari into action. Cam would be there in another moment. She couldn't let him be alone with whomever, *whatever,* she'd just seen. She didn't make it two steps past the doorway when she saw two shadows coming down the stairs.

"Is anyone hurt?" She heard Mr. Everly before she saw him.

Carissa turned to allow the men to exit the building.

"No, Fudge pulled Mrs. Harbridge away in time," Jane answered. She'd made her way to the doorway now.

Hurried footsteps crunching on gravel pulled everyone's eyes to Cam, who had made his way from the rampart down into the keep and out of it. He was breathing heavily but tried to hide it by steadying his breath as he walked toward them.

"Did you see anything while you were up there?" Mr. MacLir asked.

"No." Cam shook his head. "I think it may have just been some of the old stones that haven't been cleared away yet." Carissa pulled her hands into fists at her side as he spoke. She closed her eyes and concentrated on extinguishing the elf-light that had begun to glow from her palms. Her heart instinctively pumped the elf-light to her hands sometimes. She wished she had better control of her magic.

"If this place is unsafe, we should leave," Carissa suggested once she'd regained her composure.

"Yes," Mr. MacLir agreed. His eyes surveyed the courtyard. "I think it best to leave and send a team to ensure the safety of the grounds before any celebrations are planned."

Cam didn't really need to state his agreement, but he did. He also didn't need to put an arm on Carissa's shoulder to nudge her toward the gate. Though, she had somewhat frozen in place. And she was glad to see he was all right.

No one had been harmed. The rest of the group had already cleared the premises and made their way back to the vehicles. Carissa could see the two older women squabbling and poor Jane trying to mediate.

"It's not anyone's fault. It fell from the top of the building," Jane was saying.

"That's her story." Mrs. Harbridge hugged her arms and leaned against the Everly's car.

This caused Fudge to inch closer and gesture for her to get off the expensive automobile. She pushed herself away and bent in Mrs. Alcott's direction. "Maybe you didn't throw the stone, but you probably wished it on me. And I didn't even throw that pebble at you!"

Mrs. Alcott, who was standing still and looking white as a ghost, didn't take her eyes off the castle. She was staring above the ramparts, at the top of the keep. Had she seen the specter too?

"I believe you," she said softly. "Now I know it wasn't you."

"Good." Patsy Harbridge's triumphant snort was not the last word.

"There was something there," Mrs. Alcott said. "There was someone up there who threw that stone."

So, she had seen the same thing Carissa had. Cari kept walking beside Cam, now fighting the elf-light tingling under her skin.

Patsy rolled her eyes. "Of course, there was." She dismissed the statement and threw a frustrated look at Jane.

Jane wasn't taking it as lightly. "Someone else? Did you see who?"

"I'm sure Mrs. Alcott didn't mean to imply your father or Mr. MacLir." Mrs. Harbridge couldn't have sent a clearer message. The dagger-throwing look caused her target to appear shocked.

Cam and Cari joined them, with Cam saying, "So sorry about that, ladies." He glanced at the wise old man to his right, "And Fudge. I guess some of the construction still needs to be cleared out, but not to worry. We'll take care of it before we start setting up for the celebrations."

Carissa looked back at the gatehouse, realizing that she and Cam had not been followed out by the two gentlemen. Mr. Everly was just coming out of the gate right now. Where was Mr. MacLir? She couldn't see through walls, so she looked over them. No sign of the ghost or Alden. She had no indication that they were not one and the same, either. Even though she didn't know Alden well, she couldn't imagine that it had been him.

MacLir finally emerged from the gate, and the group decided to reconvene at Gooseberry, sans the Everlys. Mrs. Harbridge offered Carissa and Cameron a ride. Carissa took the opportunity while Cam set the bicycle in the trunk of the SUV to pass on the warning from Alden. She didn't expect his reaction.

Remedy and Ruins

He exhaled a disgruntled sigh. "Cari, I know you're trying to help, but, honestly, Alden always thinks something's up. Nothing actually happened and nothing will. His sister and father came here today. Did it occur to either of you that he was drawn here because he's still attached to them?"

Cari blinked in disbelief. She flinched when Cameron slammed the trunk.

"This is really important to me, Carissa. It's my first project as Ambassador to Vale. Can you please, for once, just try to be supportive?"

Supportive? Wasn't trying to save his life supportive enough? And what did he mean by "*for once*?" Carissa wanted to make an argument, but she was at a loss for words.

Cam walked around the side of the SUV without another word. Carissa turned to the other side and gave the castle one last look before taking her seat. The clouds were darkening, and she knew almost with certainty that what was yet to come was more than the threat of rain.

Chapter 6

Faeries and Foreboding

Gooseberry Bakery had nothing on the menu to settle Cari's stomach. By the time the four of them exited Mrs. Alcott's vehicle and put Cari's bicycle back in front of her shop, it was long enough for them to be noticed by Moss Hill's nosiest leprechaun. Barnaby showed up not minutes after they sat in the plump red booth by the window.

"How'd it go at the castle?" The minuscule fae lifted a red chair and dragged it over to the table.

"Barn," Cam said, "this meeting is only for the subcommittee leaders."

Barnaby held up both hands. "Don't worry, I won't whisper a word to anyone. But weren't you supposed to meet at the castle?"

Mrs. Harbridge and Mrs. Alcott, who were presently not speaking to one another and looking in opposite directions, each took this as an invitation to rant.

"We were attacked," Mrs. Alcott said simply. "Someone decided it would be fun to throw stones and make accusations."

"Who's making accusations now? And how could I have thrown that stone at you? I was on the ground with you, and it came from above."

"Some rubble fell," Cameron raised his voice above the ladies'. "Fortunately, no one was hurt."

"Thank goodness." Patsy Harbridge adjusted the pin holding her hair in place. "Though if it weren't for that butler, I don't know if that would be the case."

"I'm telling you," Mrs. Alcott leaned across the table and said in a haunting voice, "I saw something in the castle. Someone in the window threw those stones."

"Mrs. Alcott," Cameron pressed his hands flat against the table and used his most reassuring voice, "only Mr. Everly and Mr. MacLir were in the upper levels of the castle, and there's no way either of them was throwing stones."

"You're saying I'm lying?"

Cam looked at Carissa. She glanced down at her hands. She knew that wasn't the response he was looking for, but she couldn't back him up on this. She believed Rosa Alcott was right. Cam closed his eyes, took a breath, and tried again. "Maybe you thought you saw something, but you must've been mistaken."

"Not necessarily." The leprechaun squirmed in his chair, pulling himself higher up over the table. "The castle could very well be haunted. Though I wouldn't worry about it too much. It was probably just a powrie."

Carissa sat up. "A powrie?"

The leprechaun, helpful as always when it came to stories about the town, explained, "It's a harmless solitary fae, a creature that exists somewhere between the Otherworld and the world beyond." He grew more excited by the minute, earning him an increasingly threatening look from Cam. He shrunk back. "They're harmless, though. All they do is scare people by throwing the occasional stone."

Mrs. Harbridge looked as if she was going to say something, but Cameron beat her to it. "All right, let's not jump to conclusions. There were construction workers there for a month without anyone coming to harm. Even if there somehow is a powrie, we can take care of that and still hold the celebrations."

Carissa couldn't believe what she was hearing. She barely controlled her outburst. "No, you can't do that."

"Carissa," Cam said in a sharp tone she'd never heard him use before. It made her pull back, startled. Even he seemed to realize how he sounded. "Sorry." He sighed. "Can we just please do some basic planning? Even if we hold the celebration somewhere else, we still need to plan one. I have to take something to the mayor."

Carissa could see in his eyes that he was pleading for some sympathy. If she wasn't so wound up and hadn't just been ignored by him and then yelled at, she might've been more sympathetic. Right now, looking out the window was all she could do to not shout at him.

Mrs. Harbridge patted his hand twice. "You're right. It probably was just an accident." She shot dagger eyes at Mrs. Alcott so she would stop before she started another argument. "We're sorry, and we're happy to help you."

Mrs. Alcott grudgingly added, "More than happy to help."

Cam looked at Carissa, but she held her tongue. All that would have come out of it was another argument. Cameron frowned, but he didn't linger in the dismay.

"Barnaby," he said.

The leprechaun leaped from his seat. "Say no more. I'll leave you to it." He grappled with the chair, setting it back to a table nearby.

Cam immediately began the discussion with budgets, and the brainstorming began. Mrs. Harbridge and Mrs. Alcott were a treasure trove of ideas, all of which Cameron wrote down. Every time he looked up from writing, his eyes glided to Cari, his hurt evident. The more the discussion progressed, the guiltier she felt. She was here to participate. Not doing so would be shirking her responsibility. She stopped her ghoulish behavior as the conversation turned to which local businesses to include.

Knowing that it would make Maren happy, she shared an idea as the waitress came to offer drinks.

She asked the waitress, "Are you having a pumpkin carving contest the week of the All Hallows' Eve celebration?"

"We are." The waitress held the pencil to her chin and tucked her order pad under her arm. "During the holiday week, just bring your pumpkin into the bakery. We're lining the windows with them."

"Do you think you could bring them to the All Hallows' Eve celebration to do the final judging there?" Cari looked at Mrs. Alcott. "And I know I'm not in charge of foods, but what if we had a pumpkin-themed baking contest to go along with it?"

"I don't know, dear, that's a lot of pumpkin. Maybe fall-themed baked goods?" Mrs. Alcott corrected.

"Cinnamon, pecan, that sort of thing, yes, I think that's brilliant," Mrs. Harbridge agreed.

"Excellent," Cam said. He gave Cari a half-smile.

"Actually, it was Maren's idea," she said.

"Whoever's idea it was, it's a good one," Cam complimented.

He might be back to friendly appreciation, but she was not. She participated in the rest of the lunch, reminding herself that at least as long as all of them were here eating, none of them were in danger on the castle grounds. An hour later, a car came by the eatery for Cam. A new chauffeur stood outside, sent by the mayor. Cari pictured the boy in the uniform and compared him to Cam in his suit. She missed the simpler version of Cam, the one who cared more for people than politics. As they all rose to leave, Carissa gripped Cam's arm.

"We need to talk."

He put a hand up to stop her. "Cari, I know what you're going to say. I'm sorry that there was a scare at the castle grounds today, but I promise it'll be all right. We'll clear any debris and secure the area before preparations even begin."

"You don't understand. It's more than that—"

63

"The powrie, I know. I heard Barn too. I'll tell the mayor."

"You're not listening." She injected as much sternness into her voice as possible without raising her volume.

That wounded look returned. "Okay, I'm sorry. We'll talk tonight at the dinner. The mayor is waiting for me right now."

Carissa turned her face to the window, her jaw set and arms re-folding.

"We'll talk tonight." He reached a hand to her arm. "I promise."

Carissa stewed about Cameron as she watched him get into the black Mercedes. She continued stewing as she walked into the Seelie Tree Apothecary shop, and even after she took her purse from its criss-cross placement across her body and set it on the hanger in the back room.

"Cari?"

Carissa had completely ignored her assistant, who appeared at the doorway.

"What's wrong?"

Cari decided it was best not to get into it with Maren. She had a feeling she knew whom Maren would side with on the matter. Instead, she shrugged.

"Nothing." Hearing the shop bell, she walked with Maren out to the counter.

"Good afternoon, Mr. Morely," Carissa said. The customer tipped his hat, taking it off indoors.

Maren wouldn't budge, but before she could get a word out, Carissa turned to her with that same inauthentic smile she'd used with her customer.

"Gooseberry is taking the pumpkin carving competition to the castle, and we're holding a baking competition as well."

Maren's smile could have put any cartoon character's goofy grin to shame. "You are?" Her eyes drifted, clearly plotting her entry. Carissa's shoulders sunk a little. Maren took way too much stock in things like competitions than she should. As if being judged outright or comparing herself to her sister, in Maren's case, was a healthy way to determine self-worth. It wasn't, in Carissa's opinion. But she didn't say

64

anything. What, really, was the harm in a baking challenge for the festival?

Nothing if Maren won.

About two weeks of sulking if she lost.

Successful in having distracted Maren from the fact that she was angry with Cam, Carissa went on with the rest of her day. She tended to customers and listened to Maren's debate on what she'd bake and who would be a baking partner.

"You and me," Maren said. "I'm sure we could come up with something special."

"Oh no." Carissa shook her head as she locked the back door. "I'm not much of a baker, and even if I were, I don't think a subcommittee leader should be allowed to participate. It wouldn't look right."

"How about your nan? She's an excellent baker, and she's mostly retired. Do you think she'd be interested?"

"You'd have to ask her." Carissa shut the lights and opened the front door.

Maren followed. "I think I will. I'll come by tonight."

"Oh, Maren, I won't be home. I'm going to that dinner," Cari started to say.

"Your nan will be there, though, right?"

"I suppose so." Carissa took the handles of her bicycle, relenting to her friend's persistence as she undid her spell.

"Tell her I'll be there at seven." Maren waved goodbye.

Carissa enjoyed a pleasant ride for a while before the rain began to drizzle. At times like these, she could use her elf-light to ride between the raindrops, or at least part them as if the air itself were her umbrella. This required only a conscious use of magic, but the very use of it made her dark brown eyes sensitive to any magic around her.

As she passed the community garden, she could see two little veggie thieves causing a tiny squash to fly in the air as if the wind were strong enough to carry it. She stopped her bicycle, clicked the kickstand into place, and snuck up on the nature faeries. They continued without noticing her presence.

Each one glowed as the rain fell around them. The squash wobbled as the two held their hands out to keep it steady between them. Once they had it secured, they turned toward the Crescent Circle neighborhood sign as if to zoom back home but stopped abruptly as Carissa's shadow loomed over them.

Two tiny pairs of eyes looked up to see an annoyed half-elf with crossed arms and a stern expression. They faced each other, then dropped the vegetable altogether. Turning with heads down, they placed their hands behind their backs. They wouldn't be forgiven so easily.

"Cynthia, Hiya! Are you stealing from the community garden?"

The sibling sprites pointed at each other, then stuck their tongues out and finally turned their backs away from one another.

"Blaming each other now? I can't believe you two." Carissa put her palm out and scooted the nature faeries toward her bicycle. "You'll come home with me this instant, and I don't want to hear a word from either of you."

The boy and girl faeries didn't exactly have a choice, being ushered into the bicycle basket. The two just sulked and held onto the basket. Cari took the opportunity to vent.

"You'll apologize to Mrs. Harbridge, and while you're at it, apologize to Chaos, too." Carissa knew they'd be stomping or kicking or doing something to argue about Chaos, but she didn't want to see it, so she didn't look down. "Chaos has had a hard enough time adjusting to Moss Hill without you two getting on her case about her wings. The poor girl is probably scared." Now Carissa did glance at the two. "How would you feel if your wings were turning black?"

Hiya and Cynthia sat flatly on their bottoms in the basket, facing away from Carissa. All she could see was the faint glow of their magic shielding them from the rain. If they wanted to sulk in a dark basket the whole ride home, that was their problem.

Carissa probably should've left it at that, but she was so mad at Cameron, at today's events, at everything, that she kept chiding the pair.

"You two are always causing trouble. I can't let you go anywhere without finding out that you've made a mess or hurt someone's feelings or done something wrong. The garden is for everyone to share. It's Mrs. Harbridge's turn this month to divvy up the items, and she'll probably want to use the squash for the celebrations this month. She can't do that if you're stealing them."

The glow in the basket dimmed. Cari's stomach tightened, and her breathing became more labored, not entirely due to the upward slant of the hill she was traveling on. It wasn't fair. She was taking her anger out on them, and that was wrong.

When they got home, Hiya and Cynth floated out of the basket with their eyes downcast. Carissa followed them indoors, where they usually shook themselves off, making everything around them wet in one go. This time, they just dripped their way across the hall and into the kitchen where Chaos was sitting on the counter. Nan was taking out measuring bowls.

The two nature faeries stopped beside Chaos. Chaos questioned Cari with her eyes. Carissa looked away, pretending that she was unbothered and simply put her purse on the kitchen table. Out of the corner of her eye, she saw Chaos take a step toward Cynth and pat her arm, accepting her apology. Her little brows replanted themselves into understanding as they sniffled and signed their apologies.

Cynthia burst into tears and hugged Chaos. The O-shape of the little tan faerie's mouth was priceless. She froze for a second, wholly enveloped, with her arms pinned to her sides. Slowly, her tiny hand moved up to Cynth's elbow and gave another gentle pat of consolation. Then Hiya joined the group, wrapping his shoulders around the girls and wailing. Chaos's eyes closed and she flinched. She struggled to bring her other hand to Hiya's arm as well.

Despite herself, Cari laughed at the scene. This warranted three pairs of eyes narrowing on her like the pointy ends of a druid's hazel wand. But that wasn't all. Even Nan's gaze was on her from the top of her glasses. Cari cleared her throat. She put her hands on her knees and spoke over the sprites.

"I'm sorry I yelled at you. But I'm happy you're friends again." The three broke their hug. "Again" might not be the appropriate word since they never seemed to completely get along. The sniffles continued. Hiya wiped his nose.

That made her feel worse. "I'll tell you what," she said. "All three of you can help with the decorations for the All Hallows' Eve celebration as soon as we start working on them. How does that sound?"

Cynth looked at Chaos, who smiled and closed her eyes while giving her nod of approval. Hiya swirled through the air in a triumphant hurrah.

"So, what's going on in here?" Carissa eyed the measuring cup in Nan's hand.

"Your friend Maren is coming over to practice baking, apparently."

"She called you already?" Cari walked to the counter and looked at the recipe Nan had taken out. Her grandmother picked up the spatula and whacked her hand.

"Maren wants it to be a surprise. And don't you have a dinner to get ready for?"

Carissa's hands went to her hips. "It's impossible to travel faster than the news around this town."

"So, why are you still trying?" Nan waved the spatula as if to say scat.

Cari scooted all the way up to her room to prepare for the dinner at the Everly's. Two hours and three dresses later, she was ready to go. This was far longer than her normal preparation time. She usually wasn't choosy with dresses, or fussy with her fuzzy hair, but she'd never been to a party at one of the wealthiest homes in Moss Hill before.

Deep down there were likely several reasons for her preoccupation, but she was doing her best to keep those reasons from surfacing to conscious awareness. One last glance in the mirror at her calf-length, long-sleeved maroon dress assured her that the outfit she'd chosen was appropriate for a formal dinner.

She clicked the lights off, left the room, and made her way downstairs to the sounds of banging pots and laugher. She stuck her head into the kitchen. Maren was at work with a mixing bowl, a smidge of orange something on her nose. Hiya and Cynth were happily "helping" by throwing around scoops of frosting like they were snowballs.

Chaos was shaking a finger at them, but they didn't stop until she pulled Hiya by his ear. Nan, meanwhile, was missing the ruckus with her back turned as she washed dishes at the sink.

The doorbell rang, probably Cameron—right on time.

"Well, everyone looks busy here." Cari crossed into the kitchen and up to the island counter.

"Oh, no, Cari." Maren left the mixing bowl and waved her hands to shoo her. "Go to your party. You'll see what we've made when you get back."

"Fine," Carissa put her arms up in submission, "I'm going." She took a step back, and then in typical elvish fashion, she snuck a little of the orange concoction from the bowl with her finger.

Maren grabbed her by the shoulders, spun her around, and pushed her out of the kitchen. Carissa happily complied. She bounded up the step, calling out, "It's delicious!"

Her smile faded in front of the scarlet door. She stopped herself, patted her hair—done up in a twist—then sighed at how much her actions were mimicking Patsy Harbridge. She only hesitated a second or two longer, then she opened the door. There was Cameron in his black suit and dark tie, smiling at her with a rose in his hand.

"Hi," he said.

If he was uncertain whether his hello would be accepted, he was right. The problem was Cari was equally undecided whether she would forgive him for not listening to her earlier.

Astoria Wright

She took the rose and gave a skeptic smile in exchange. How the night would go remained to be seen.

Chapter 7

Dinner Guests and Guile

The Everlys spared no expense. Fudge came to the door in full uniform with his pasty hair slicked back. Cameron greeted him with his usual warmth and was met with Fudge's usual lack of it. They crossed the polished foyer, and Cari peeked into the living room where several guests had already gathered.

Fudge took her coat, and she and Cameron stepped farther inside. Autumn floral decorations in every niche added a holiday feel to the occasion, from the purple asters to the orange marigolds. A massive fire flickered far across the expanse.

"Carissa, Cameron, I'm so glad you're here," Jane Everly greeted them, as did the cold, courteous smiles of Mr. and Mrs. Everly. The warm hug from Jane made up for it.

Carissa noticed that Jane was wearing the gold pendant with the intricately carved tree on it. It was one she hadn't seemed fond of before, but it was beautiful against the lace bodice of her midnight purple evening gown. Carissa complimented her on it.

Jane's hand rested on the necklace, and a shadow passed over her face. Cari noted the odd gesture, but the sullen look passed as they moved farther into the room. Jane smiled again and held a palm out toward the crowd.

"Please, come in. I'd like you to meet—" Jane dropped her hand and swerved this way and that, searching the room. Her eyes settled back on Carissa. "I'm not sure where our guest of honor has gone, but you're welcome to mingle. I have more guests to greet."

Carissa and Cam nodded as Jane excused herself. Before walking any farther, Carissa took another moment to admire the welcoming atmosphere. Not only was the room lively with conversation, but the dishes being prepared in the kitchens filled the home with the fragrance of savory spices directly followed by the hint of apricot cobbler. Carissa closed her eyes, taking it in. A hand on her back brought her out of the trance.

"I'll get us some drinks." Cam removed his arm and looked around the impossibly large living room for a bar or snack table. No sooner did he say that when Fudge appeared beside her with a tray of champagne glasses. Cam was already gone from her sight. She took one and thanked the butler, then began an exploration of the room.

Carissa walked past several conversations, tilting her head to acknowledge this person or that as they said hello. None were close acquaintances, and none were holding topics of conversation that she particularly wanted to join. She spotted Cameron conversing with the mayor. She took a sip of the fizzy drink and swallowed her disappointment.

Deeper and deeper into the crowd, which seemed to grow with new arrivals every second, she noted that the room seemed to make an L-shape, then a U as it curved around the home. Just before the empty dining room, she stopped, realizing she'd gone too far. She turned back around, which brought her face to face with Magnus MacLir.

He stood with one hand in the pocket of his navy cashmere suit, and one hand holding his drink. Carissa's first reaction was to look awkwardly at the floor. Then, deciding to act like a normal person, she lifted her gaze to meet Mr. MacLir's and extended a hand to introduce herself.

"Hello, sir, I'm Carissa Shae."

He met her with a firm handshake. "The owner of the Seelie Tree Apothecary. I'm sorry we haven't formally met before." His grasp relaxed, but he hesitated before letting go of her hand. "You look surprised, but I'm sure you know my name by now as well."

"Mr. Magnus MacLir. You're well known around this town, but I'm surprised you know who I am."

"I've had my eye on Moss Hill for a while now. It's quite literally my business to know this town inside and out." MacLir took a sip of his drink, then motioned with a nod back toward the main room.

She followed him, asking, "I'm curious, what made you think of Moss Hill in the first place? Did Mayor Belkin reach out to your company, or did something else spark your interest in our little town?" Cari was thinking of Nan's comment, wondering about what had made the fae agree to the tourism and whether Mayor Belkin had only opened Moss Hill up to the unseelie. The possibility of exposing some darker purpose made it seem bold to be asking the question.

If MacLir was aware of anything nefarious, he didn't show it. In fact, he seemed amused by the question, smiling with radiantly white teeth. "You've been outside Moss Hill for your education, is that right?"

Cari nodded.

"Do you remember what your 'little town' looks like from the ferry coming here?"

Carissa thought back. She gripped her glass, trying to remember, but there was very little to recall. "I'm afraid I didn't see it on a good day. It was foggy when I came back from college. I didn't visit on breaks, so I only saw it just the once coming home."

"Mmm." The monosyllable response showed understanding. They came back to the fireplace where

MacLir set his glass by the mantle. "The fog is a common thing. But if you're often traveling, some days you catch it at the right angle and there it is, so beautiful it has to be," he met her eyes directly as he said the last word, "otherworldly."

Cari nearly dropped the glass. Could this man know about Moss Hill's fae population? Did he believe Reginald, or would John have told him? Or worse, was he like John? His choice of wording couldn't be coincidence, of that she was convinced. Her discussion with MacLir was interrupted by a voice carrying over the crowd with greater volume than would be deemed proper for a party.

"Lost at sea, indeed. A man goes traveling and the first opportunity his fellow citizens have to snatch up his property, he takes." It was Mr. O'Brien standing around a coffee table with his wife, Mayor Belkin, Cam, and Tilly Brier. She wasn't a subcommittee leader for the festival, and Cari would not have been surprised if she was here solely as a reporter.

"Eamon, we didn't know you were still alive. The fact of the matter is that your wife renounced her claim on the castle," the mayor replied.

"Only because of the legal battle she didn't want to fight with you and the MacAirts."

Mary O'Brien reddened at her husband's words.

"Why the MacAirts?" Tilly asked. The reporter in her twitched her fingers as she clutched her purse. Cari knew she was just waiting to write all this down.

"On several occasions, the senior Mr. O'Brien said that he would leave the estate to his daughter's family." Mayor Belkin seemed unperturbed, but Carissa noted how tightly his meaty fingers were grasping the champagne glass in his hands.

"That is nothing but hearsay," O'Brien said. "The MacAirts had no legal claim to the estate."

"Be that as it may, with no updated will in your father's files—and you being gone—the estate went to probate. MacAirt's only child, Mrs. Arin Everly, and your wife, Mary, mutually agreed to allow the castle to become the property of the town of Moss Hill as a historical monument. We've already begun renovations." Mayor Belkin's frustration was becoming more audible.

"And you'll finish them over my dead body." O'Brien's anger sharpened his tongue.

"Out of courtesy," Cam interjected, "we've halted renovations until this matter is settled. We never meant to upset the previous owners." Cameron meant it well, but his word choice had not helped matters.

"Previous owners." O'Brien scowled. "The paper you're basing that on is not a valid one without my signature. I'll contest it in court if I have to."

The mayor held his hands up, smiling. "Come now, Mr. O'Brien. Let's not talk about courts. We're all friends here. It doesn't matter to me who holds the deed. What matters is that the castle is restored for all to see. We've nearly completed restoration—free of charge to you. Once you see the work that's been done, you'll be glad of it, I'm sure. The castle will bring in much more than was spent on it, enough for the town to get back what it spent on it and for you to profit if your claim is valid. So, you see, nothing has been lost."

The mayor must have known O'Brien's claims were credible. He snuck in that word "if your claim is valid" between sentences quickly enough to be overlooked. The mayor put a hand on Eamon O'Brien's shoulder. O'Brien only scoffed.

"Open to tourists, indeed! My father's wish was to share that castle with Moss Hill, not the whole world." O'Brien stepped within inches of Mayor Belkin's face. "There are things in that castle not fit for any but a Mossie to see."

"Mr. O'Brien," Cam leaned to his side to set his glass on the coffee table. By the looks of it, he hadn't taken one sip. "I respect your reservations about opening the castle to the public; however, plans are currently underway to hold an All Hallows' Eve celebration on the castle grounds. We had planned to invite the people of Vale to join us. I'm sure you wouldn't object to a celebration between Mossies and the fae as a way of strengthening our good relations with them."

Mr. O'Brien's lips pursed, considering. During his lack of response, Cameron's eyes flickered over to Carissa, standing in silence with MacLir, watching the interaction. Cameron waved her over.

"Mr. O'Brien, you remember Carissa Shea from the Seelie Tree Apothecary, don't you?"

Cari looked at MacLir, who smiled amusedly as she left his company to join the group. As a non-Mossie, MacLir must be wondering about their internal disputes, especially after his strange encounter with that tourist. But he didn't seem as interested in things as he was entertained by them. Mr. and Mrs. Everly stopped to chat with him, and Cari could see him sipping his wine with a casual hand in his pocket. She heard him exchanging pleasantries with his hosts before she made her way over to Cameron.

O'Brien's face flickered with recognition. "Carissa Shae, Nessa's granddaughter? You were still in college when I went away. Never came home for a visit. I remember Nessa being bothered by that. She spent plenty of time worrying about you, guess she didn't need to." The two shook hands, Carissa less enthusiastically than Eamon.

Nan was bothered that she hadn't come home on breaks? She'd never said that. She was always supportive of her venturing around the UK on breaks or taking those summer classes to get her degree faster. It didn't sound like her at all to have been distressed. But it seemed like a funny thing to lie about.

Nan had always described Mr. O'Brien—all the O'Briens, in fact—as very likable, upstanding folks. They weren't ones to exaggerate or gossip. Either he knew her nan better than Cari did, or Nan's picture of the O'Briens wasn't what she truly thought.

Eventually, the mayor was able to sway Mr. O'Brien to other topics, with some help from Father Quinn, who asked about his journeys in the last few years. The disagreeable sneer lingered on Mr. O'Brien's face, but his wife chimed in.

"His boat was set adrift and left him stranded, but in the most wondrous of places—"

"Mary," he stopped her, "they've no need to hear all that. Let's just say that I've seen enough of the world to realize how big it truly can be and leave it at that."

Carissa sipped her drink, wondering. He claimed the world was big but was so concerned by a small plot of it in the form of Fairfield Castle. Mr. MacLir had a different take on it.

"Adventures, what interesting things to hear about and terrible things to live. Nothing makes one appreciate home so much as an adventure."

Carissa would have returned to a conversation with the enigmatic Mr. MacLir, but he'd been cornered by a somewhat intrigued-looking group of ladies. Even Mrs. Alcott, a widow for nearly the last ten years, fussed with her hair while eyeing the stranger. She seemed to catch herself and blushed when she saw Carissa. She left MacLir's admirers to speak with Carissa.

"That O'Brien's not quite like his father, is he?" she said, switching the topic to the heated exchange they'd just witnessed. "The old mayor was less interested in properties and more invested in the people living in them."

As far as Cari knew, no one had ever lived in the castle. She knew Mrs. Alcott meant it metaphorically, but it made her wonder. "When was the last time anyone lived in the castle?"

"Long ago," Mrs. Alcott said. "Since before Moss Hill was even a town."

"Why didn't Mayor O'Brien restore the castle like Belkin is doing now?"

Mrs. Alcott put her hand to her chin. "I don't know. I'm sure he had his reasons. Perhaps he hadn't thought of it."

Or perhaps he hadn't wanted to even consider it, Cari thought. While she didn't agree with Reginald's belief that their island was really Hy Brasil, Carissa knew Moss Hill well enough that she was convinced there was more going on beneath its surface.

***

Carissa was famished by the time dinner rolled around. The dishes were exquisite, a mouthwatering menu of five courses, six if you counted the hors d'oeuvres Fudge had passed around before dinner. The butler was a curiosity. There was obviously a chef, aside from Fudge, and a waitress helping him to serve the entrées. But aside from that, Carissa hadn't seen a host of servers this evening. Fudge did well to fade into the background so that most of the time he went unnoticed, but Cari picked up on the hint of magic he was using throughout the night. He was impossibly quick, appearing at the moment a request was mentioned. Fudge served the dinner so that it appeared slow and calm, but nearly all the guests had their soups and salads, entrées and desserts in what seemed like seconds of each other. No one but Carissa seemed to notice and that, she assumed, was because she had the same elf-magic he was using. No elf would make themselves a servant in someone else's home. She had to assume, then, that he was something similar to an elfkin, like Sal. The Everlys probably knew exactly what he was, the Mossies likely didn't care if they did see anything odd, but did Mr. MacLir notice? The Everlys didn't seem to think that was an issue to fret about, what with Fudge using his magic so openly in front of everyone.

Carissa tried to ignore it. If they didn't care, what business was it of hers? Instead, she allowed herself to enjoy the sautéed sirloin, the roasted veggies covered in a dill sauce baked inside a pumpkin, the apricot cobbler, and coffee with a hint of pecan in the froth. It was easy to overindulge, which she might have done even more if the conversation hadn't been so captivating.

During the first course, Mr. MacLir mentioned the exquisite decoration on the wall above the chair at the head of the table. Cari and the other guests looked up to see what looked like a tree branch, only it was silver with gold apples growing out of it. The sculpture, for that's what Carissa assumed it was, had been crafted by a true master of the arts. It looked so vivid and lifelike, she could've sworn it was a real branch. Cari could hardly take her eyes off it.

Mr. MacLir asked, "I think everyone at this table is curious to know what that is, how you came about it, and why you keep it in your dining hall. We, or at least I, would like to hear the story."

All eyes moved to Mr. Everly, who was not surprised by the question. He dabbed his napkin on his mouth and looked to his wife. "You'll have to ask Arin."

Arin Everly spoke to her daughter. "Jane, dear, you tell it."

Jane appeared taken aback, her eyes darting around the table at the guests. Then she brought her napkin to her lips and set it back on her lap.

"The branch is a symbol of my mother's family. Her maiden name is MacAirt." Jane cleared her throat and continued, less timidly, "A long time ago, the legend is that my ancestor, Cormac, saw a man on a hill carrying this branch." Cari didn't miss how her eyes glanced at MacLir for a moment. "He was instantly captivated by it and asked the stranger what the branch did.

"'It can heal anything,' the stranger said. 'And the golden apples will always be replenished.'

"At that moment, Cormac desired the branch above anything. He and the stranger became friends, and Cormac eventually asked him for the branch, to which the stranger agreed he could have it. But in return, the stranger asked for three favors. He didn't say what they were at the time. Later, he returned to the hill on three separate occasions to collect each favor. The first time, he asked for Cormac's daughter to come away with him. The second time, his son. The third, his wife."

"What a monstrous thing to ask." MacLir laughed, picked up his glass, and leaned back into his chair. "Surely Cormac wouldn't have allowed that!"

Jane held an expressionless gaze on the guest of honor until the silence was uncomfortable enough for Mrs. Alcott to speak up, "Well, did he or didn't he?"

"Yes," MacLir set his glass down. "Tell us the rest."

Jane went on, this time her eyes met the guests' rather than avoiding them. "The branch would cause people to sleep and heal any kind of pain, including memories of loss or grief. MacAirt's people knew much of grief, and to help them all, he was willing to trade anything. Or so he thought. MacAirt allowed the stranger to take away his family and used the branch to cause any who loved them to sleep and forget their pain upon waking. But it didn't work on MacAirt himself, and the grief of losing his family was too much, so he eventually went after the stranger."

"And did he find him?" Mrs. Harbridge asked.

"Yes," Jane, growing more confident in outward appearance, did not hesitate with her response. "The stranger took him to the world beyond life where he showed him many wonders. After teaching him a lesson about greed and wisdom, he allowed Cormac to return to the land of the living and restored his family to him. It was said that Cormac was wiser than anyone in his family before him after that experience."

"Fascinating," MacLir said. "How wonderful it would be to see things like that today. Faerie magic!" MacLir shook his head, taking the last bite of his apricot cobbler. "Can you imagine?"

Naturally, every Mossie at the table showed discomfort in their own ways. Some exchanged glances, some squirmed in their chairs, and most looked at the Everlys, anticipating more from them.

Father Quinn settled the matter. "I think we can all agree greatest magic is in the heart, and *that* we have plenty of in Moss Hill."

"Here-here," Mr. Everly toasted to that.

Remedy and Ruins

Not long after, Mrs. Everly called on Fudge to clear the table. She pushed her plate back and announced, "Why don't we adjourn to the back garden?"

The lighted yard and ocean views were breathtaking. But Carissa was overly full and getting tired. She gave Cameron's arm a light tug and told him she was ready to leave almost as soon as they stepped onto the patio.

"One minute." Cam held a finger up and walked away from her. He found Mr. O'Brien on the grass near the rose bushes. Carissa's anger flared as she watched, though she couldn't hear what they were saying. Her arms crossed and she was this close to a foot-tapping display of annoyance, except that Cam seemed to end his conversation by reaching out for a handshake. Mr. O'Brien nodded as if in agreement with whatever Cameron had said but either missed or dismissed his outstretched hand. Cam left, awkwardly turning the rejected gesture into a wave. Then he rejoined Cari on the steps, and they said their goodbyes to the hosts.

Jane wasn't in sight, but at least they'd made an exit with the Everlys. Carissa even managed a show of happy satisfaction with the dinner party, which she kept on her face until they made it to the driveway and into Cameron's car.

"Great night, wasn't it?" Cam glanced at her from the wheel.

She stared out the window.

"I said—"

"I heard," Carissa replied.

"You're angry about something?"

Cari stared at him. Cam's dumbfounded expression suggested he wasn't getting it.

"You're angry *at me* for something?" Cam corrected.

"Not angry," Carissa corrected further, "annoyed."

"Not much of an improvement," Cam said.

"Cam," she turned, so her body was facing him, "why are you so bent on having the party at the castle?"

Cam let out a frustrated groan. "Not this again. Cari, I told you on the way up here that the mayor sent some people to investigate. They didn't find anything. The rubble falling was likely an accident, and it was probably Alden you saw at the top of the keep."

"Don't you find it suspicious that Mr. O'Brien doesn't seem to want the castle to be used by Moss Hill for anything?"

"I already told Mr. O'Brien that the decorating committee was going to start on the castle this weekend. He agreed, just now, in the garden. The condition is that we keep to the courtyard and the great hall, which I agree with since the rest of the castle is still in ruins. In fact, he's coming the first night to take a look and make sure everything is safe."

Cari raised an eyebrow.

"What?" Cam asked.

She sat back in the seat. "The whole thing just seems odd."

"Look, Cari, if you want, we can still talk to the sidhe guard."

"No," Cari said quickly. She recalled how, months ago, Alden had said that the sidhe were the only beings powerful enough to banish him if they wanted. It was risky bringing the sidhe into anything when Alden was involved. "No, it's all right. Alden wasn't even sure there was anything wrong. Maybe I'm worrying for nothing. It's just...something doesn't feel right."

Cam smiled. "It'll all go well, you'll see."

Carissa glanced out the window at the mountain. She could see the castle in the dark better than he could. With her elfish eyes, she saw a lot of things other Mossies missed. Unfortunately, that didn't mean she could see everything.

Chapter 8

Castles and Curses

If Cari had been certain that an unseen force had thrown that stone at Mrs. Alcott, she would have never agreed to the decoration committee setting foot on the castle grounds. Since she couldn't be sure that it really was a fae, and since Cameron was refusing to acknowledge that as a possibility, she had no choice but to go along with the plan as it stood. She was uneasy all afternoon on Friday though, looking over her shoulder constantly as they began decorating the castle.

There were more people here today than she thought there would be. Fae and human volunteers divvied up areas all around the courtyard. Some walked around with Mrs. Harbridge, discussing the activities they would set up closer to the event date. Sheridan shared his vision of the haunted house they'd make of the great hall and eastern side of the castle.

With all the people around, a nagging dread took up residence in the back of Carissa's mind. Having the nature faeries with her made her even more nervous, but they stayed close by on her orders. Hiya and Cynth hovered over the fall-themed flowers as Carissa planted them by the entrance gate.

The plants bloomed from the sprites' nature magic, and Carissa appreciated the fact that the three of them seemed to be getting along.

"A little to the left," Mrs. Alcott's voice rang out from the middle of the courtyard. Carissa looked up to see two short volunteers, Clancy and Barnaby, setting the banner into place. Carissa had gone with "Hallows to All this Eve-ning" as a play on words. It probably wasn't the most original, but it worked well enough. They'd position one facing inward and one outward as a welcome to Mossies and fae folk.

Cari heard Mr. O'Brien and Cam entering through the gate beside her.

"...Shoddy work of it. The old brick was better, though your workers might not have had the sense to keep any of it. I'm not impressed," O'Brien was saying. He didn't so much as glance around the courtyard but walked straight ahead like a man with a purpose.

Cam exchanged a glance with Carissa. His face was getting redder by the second, and his eyes exceeded any annoyance Carissa had shown the night before. He took a breath and said as calmly and flatly as she'd ever heard him before, "Sir, once you see the brickwork from the top of the rampart, I'm sure you'll change your mind."

"I very much doubt it. I've half a mind to cancel the celebrations altogether. Whose harebrained idea was it to hold a celebration here?"

Carissa didn't hear Cameron's answer before they were out of earshot. She didn't even want to eavesdrop on that argument but caught snippets right up until they walked into the castle. Cam had been working hard on the planning all week, and Mr. O'Brien was throwing insults at him like a dartboard. Once they disappeared inside the great hall, Carissa's full attention went back to the flowers.

She looked down at the perennials to see Chaos twirling across three of the flower pots at once. Her faerie magic sparkled behind her, sprinkling down to the flora below. Cari smiled as she waited for the effect. Her happy expression faded when she saw the magic at work. The plants didn't just wilt, they blackened and dried up as a result of Chaos's touch.

The little sprite gasped and put her hands to her cheeks. Carissa could only imagine that this was connected to her darkening wings, which by now were half black. Chaos began to cry. Thankfully, instead of teasing, Hiya and Cynth flew to her side and put their arms on her shoulders to comfort her. Hiya brought the plant back to life. The problem was the plants, though restored, now had black edges to them. Carissa had never seen anything like it before. It seemed to make Chaos feel worse. Cari knelt beside the disheartened sprite.

"It's all right, Chaos. They're fine this way. In fact, they look even scarier like this. I'm sure everyone will love it." Chaos wiped her nose and sniffled, looking at her questioningly. Cynthia nodded, reassuring her friend that Carissa was right. Hiya, meanwhile, was scratching his head and staring at the plants, still probably wondering how on earth this had happened. "Do you think you could make some more?" Carissa asked.

Chaos looked at Cynthia and Hiya, who gave her a thumbs up, and the three nature faeries took off around the entire bunch that Cari had brought. Carissa laughed.

When the nature faeries weren't looking, though, she brought her hand to her lips and examined the flowers. She'd never seen a nature faerie do anything like this. Did this have something to do with the chocolate cosmos plant or was it something more?

"Hey, Cari, do you see this?" Maren walked up to her, holding a potted Gaillardia Kobold, also known as a goblin flower.

The red flowers with yellow tips had become black flowers with jagged tips of red- and yellow-like fire. It was as if someone had set the plant ablaze and the fire itself had been seared into it. Maren marveled at it.

"It's amazing," she said.

"You can thank the nature faeries." Carissa tried to sound unalarmed. More of the flowers changed colors across the courtyard. The volunteers admired the sprites' handiwork. Carissa moved a strand of her hair away and surveyed the plants they'd lined around the courtyard; something was definitely wrong with Chaos.

In addition to the now eerie flora, Cameron and Mr. O'Brien came into view. They were clear on the other side of the courtyard on top of the rampart walls, near the part of the castle that was still in ruins. Carissa clutched her garden shear. Her brain screamed *danger*, but then she reminded herself that the rubble had been cleared away. The two of them should be safe. Safe from physical harm, anyway.

Mental frustration might still be plaguing the two. Their body language, Cam's hands at his sides and Mr. O'Brien's quick hand gestures, made it evident that their argument had followed them upstairs. They walked through a part of the wall with a wooden enclosure and out the other side, passing two shorter figures.

One sat on the edge of the castle wall while the other pulled him back. What were they doing in the unsafe part of the castle walls, anyway? Clancy might have thought it was fun to live on the edge, but Cari knew Barnaby didn't feel that way.

Cari didn't have to use elf-magic to hear what they were saying. She could imagine it well enough. Clancy was either drunk or just being careless, Barnaby probably scolding him for sitting so high above the ground with no care about falling.

She had half a mind to go up there and pull that clurichaun by his red cap and pointy ears, but Barn seemed to have it under control. He'd gotten his cousin to stand up at any rate. Cari had to shield her eyes and squint to see them at that point since the setting sun was casting a haze over the wall.

They really should get to packing up soon. Carissa looked around her, more than half the flowers were planted. The volunteers were clearly amazed by their new black sheen. She could probably get them all planted, with a little help from her elf side, if she picked up the pace. She was a bit distracted, however, when she didn't see Chaos or the other two faeries anywhere nearby.

"Chaos?" she called. "Cynth? Where are you guys?"

She stepped outside the gate, looking over the field, and gasped. All the gorse had gone from bright yellow to black as far as the eye could see. Carissa had never even heard of a single nature faerie who could do that—let alone by themselves. Hiya and Cynth were close to the entrance. They were slowly following behind and panting, looking exhausted from trying to catch up with her.

"Where is she?" Carissa asked when she found them.

They responded by clutching each other, looks of terror on their faces. It was an odd response that made Cari tilt her head in confusion until her elf ears picked up on the sounds of screaming coming from the castle.

First one, then two screams, then a flurry of panicked voices and fear. It zapped her heart like an electric shock and curled the hair on her neck. She immediately turned, not even fighting the fae magic that was instinctually surging through her blood. Her whole body tingled with elf-light as she ran inside the castle walls.

A crowd had gathered on the ground near where Clancy and Barnaby had been. She looked up to see the two shorter figures peering over the walls, clutching the merlons for dear life. Beside them, a man was standing at the top of the wall looking down.

Due to the glare of the falling sun, she couldn't make out who the man was, but she knew immediately what the cause of the commotion was even before she could see what had everyone's attention. A sick feeling moved through her and froze her all at once.

There was one man left on the top of that wall.

There should've been two.

Chapter 9
Caught Red-Handed

"I don't know." Cameron ran a hand through his disheveled brown hair. "One minute he was standing beside me, the next he was falling."

The crowd of Mossies gathered into City Hall were not sure what to make of anything that had happened at the castle. The scene earlier had been cleared. Mr. O'Brien had been rushed to a hospital and an emergency town meeting was called by the terrified Mossies, led by Mrs. Alcott. Mr. Belkin was still in his office and, interestingly enough, so was Mr. MacLir, who was currently watching the panic in perfect calm.

"That's twice now that someone has been hurt on the castle grounds. This time seriously," Mrs. Alcott said. "Those ruins should be declared unsafe and the festival moved."

That was exactly what Carissa had told Cameron, but she wasn't saying it now. In the current moment, she was just grateful that Cam was alive and worried that angry Mossies might turn into mad mobs. She was thankful Maren had taken the sprites home. Especially when the crowd left and everyone noticed that the field of gorse flowers had been turned black.

"I'm telling you, it's an evil spirit." Mrs. Alcott was adamant. At least she wasn't blaming Cam.

Mr. Morely, who had turned out to help at Mrs. Alcott's request, said, "I think I can help. I saw the person who did it."

All eyes moved to him.

"I couldn't see the person clearly, but I saw the arms reaching out to push O'Brien from the wall. And there was one other distinguishing feature."

Carissa inched forward in her chair, as several others around her were doing.

"Don't keep us in suspense," MacLir spoke for the group. "Out with it."

Mr. Morely looked sideways at this bold newcomer. It was odd that he was allowed in on this meeting at all. Did the mayor not understand that an event like this should be a private matter for Mossies only?

Mr. Morely continued, "He was wearing a red cap."

Slowly, all eyes turned. The only person they all knew who regularly wore a red cap wasn't present. His cousin was present instead. He nearly knocked his chair down getting out of it. His eyes wildly searched the room for understanding.

"You're wrong. I was with Clancy the whole time. He didn't push anyone."

"He pushed you down twice!" one Mossie shouted.

"I saw him stumbling away!" hollered another.

Several Mossies concurred that Clancy was to blame.

"Call that troublemaker here and have him confess." Mr. Morely found enough consensus in the crowd that Mayor Belkin was now standing up to calm them from dragging out Clancy themselves.

"All right, I've heard your witnesses and Mr. Larke, and I will investigate. You can be sure that we'll handle the matter."

"In the interest of keeping things thorough," a man with bright blond hair said. "You haven't heard all the witnesses. Or, actually, all of the witnesses are leaving something out."

Carissa recognized this man from the volunteer dinner the night before. Parker, that was his name.

Carissa felt that dread wrap around her lungs. She dared not take a breath. She wasn't sure what was coming but was fairly certain it couldn't be good.

"I'm sure it's nothing, but I'm sorry, Cam, I have to mention it," Parker said.

Cameron's eyes widened.

"Mr. O'Brien was arguing with Cameron Larke, we could hear him from the top of the wall threatening to cancel everything—the celebrations, the plans for reconstruction, even the tourism. He was pretty angry."

"You're not suggesting that I pushed Mr. O'Brien?" Cam's voice was more shock than anger, though when he stood up, his chair slid back with force. "I wouldn't do that. I couldn't. You should all know me better than that." His eyes accused everyone in sight until they rested on Cari, where they lingered as if pleading for her to believe him.

"Really," Mrs. Harbridge sat on her chair, legs crossed and arms holding her seat. She pushed herself up and turned to the crowd. "This is getting out of hand. Soon you'll be accusing Mr. O'Brien of pushing himself."

Carissa knew her statement was motivated by Cameron's agreement to allow advertisements for local shops like hers to show as sponsors for the various booths and games in the event. She might also believe his innocence, but self-interest always played a minor role in Mrs. Harbridge's mind.

"Thank you, Patsy." Mayor Belkin waved a palm for her to sit. "We'll have our best officers look into the case." Wearily, he looked at Cameron. "Mr. Larke will not be a part of the investigation."

Cam parted his lips, but the stern eyes of the mayor caused them to shut. He sat, heatedly, back into his chair.

"Shouldn't the people of Vale be invited to investigate as well?" Mr. MacLir, still leaning back in his chair as if this was all a matter of mild interest, shocked the town by his statement. "The castle is on mutual ground at the border of Vale, and this lovely woman," he gestured toward Mrs. Alcott, "mentioned a *mysterious* figure whom she didn't recognize. Perhaps they'll know who it is?"

Cari's suspicion that he knew exactly who the people of Vale were was growing. Mayor Belkin put a handkerchief to his forehead and dabbed thrice.

"Yes, well, if it becomes necessary, we'll do so." The mayor cleared his throat and smiled at the crowd. "If any of you have further information or questions, please give your names to my secretary and don't worry about a thing. We have it under control."

It wasn't reassuring, especially because the "it" that was under control was currently an imagined monster in everyone's mind, changing and growing as the crowd sat there whispering.

"I saw it, it had red eyes."

"The red cap cinches it. That clurichaun has been on the edge for years."

"No offense to Cam, but if he's a suspect, he ought to be kept out of City Hall, at least while the investigation is happening." That last one was that blond-haired fellow talking with Mr. Belkin directly, in earshot of a stewing Cameron.

But it was the next comment she heard that caused Cari to freeze.

"...Skeleton. I'm telling you, I think it was the ankou."

Carissa looked around, searching for the voice who'd said that. She wasn't able to see who it was, but she caught a glimpse of Tilly writing on a notepad. The rising star of reporting stood up, grabbed her coat, and put it on without even looking at Cam. How could she be so...unaffected? Her expression was perfectly calm right up to the moment she put a hand on Cam's arm and gave him a sympathetic look. Then, intrigue no doubt guiding her step, she walked toward the door, exchanging a few words with the blond-haired man as they walked out the door.

It boiled Cari's blood. For the second time that night she felt her elf-light tingling in her hands, though the motivation was different. She calmed her rage and rose from her chair, intending to offer genuine sympathy and help to her friend.

Cam was sitting miserably in his chair when she walked up. The second her shadow passed over him, he looked up. Then, without a word, he sprang from his seat and took her hand, walking briskly out the door.

"You know I'm innocent," he said when they were outside.

"Of course." Cari had never seen Cam so upset. Her eyes briefly swayed to Tilly and Parker talking over by a tree. The conversation ended and Tilly headed back toward them.

Cam looked to the side, following her eyes. "That's Parker Greer. He's been trying to ruin me since he started working at City Hall. He's just hoping I get charged for this."

"Parker? The blond man? I've never heard you talk about him."

"He's from Moss Hill's east side. He comes from money. His parents own the Failte."

The *Failte Abhaile*, pronounced fall-cha ah-ball-yeh, meaning "welcome home," was the largest and only hotel in Moss Hill. It was often shortened to the Failte, but it was never short of compliments. In addition to being a hotel, it boasted the fanciest restaurant and event center on the island. Before tourism had expanded, it had thrived on weddings and events alone but had been doing extremely well since the island had seen more visitors.

Maren had gone on one date with Parker months ago. From what Maren had recalled, he was a rude, spoiled stereotype of a rich snob. Carissa kept that information to herself. In fact, she deliberately said nothing until Tilly passed them as she made her way back indoors.

When Tilly was gone, Cameron added, "Parker thought he should have the position of liaison to Vale."

"Don't worry." Carissa put a hand on Cam's shoulder. "We'll prove it wasn't you."

Cam put his own hand on hers, and they stood like that a moment. Mary O'Brien came up to them with a handkerchief in her hands. Her eyes were watering and red.

"Excuse me." The woman's breath hitched as she asked, "Do you know where I could find Mayor Belkin?"

Cam and Carissa both pointed to the door they'd just come from. Carissa gave a gentle squeeze and let go of Cameron's shoulder, offering to show Mrs. O'Brien directly to the meeting room, which was all still full of frightened Mossies.

"Mrs. O'Brien." The mayor walked to the woman, reaching to hold both of her hands in his. "I'm so sorry about what happened. How is he?"

"He's unconscious," she said. "The doctors say he's in a coma." The room was still while she explained, except for MacLir.

"He's in the hospital, and yet you've come here. What's happened to make you travel all this way?" MacLir was not shy about asking questions, Cari was quickly learning.

He was right, too. Mrs. O'Brien wiped her nose and nodded. Then she lowered her voice, though she needn't have bothered. Mossies had good ears for gossip and any who couldn't hear her would only get the news later from someone who had.

"He spoke before he slipped into his sleep. He said two words." She took a moment to compose herself as she fought back the tears. It felt like an eternity before she revealed her husband's last utterance, "Red cap."

***

By the time Carissa had left City Hall, everyone who'd stayed was convinced it was Clancy who'd pushed Mr. O'Brien. Barnaby had fled faster than she could catch up with him. Carissa wanted to assure him that she didn't believe it for a second. Cari didn't know Clarence well, but Barnaby she trusted completely. If he said his cousin was innocent, she had no reason to doubt him. Clancy might be a drunkard, but no one in Moss Hill had ever accused him of being violent. Mischievous, maybe, but violent?

Besides that, something had thrown the stones at Mrs. Alcott and Mrs. Harbridge the other day, and the clurichaun had definitely not been there.

On her way to her bicycle, Mrs. O'Brien stopped her. "Cari!" The woman's voice shook with tears. "I wanted to ask you...."

Cari put a hand on Mrs. O'Brien's arm. Though her husband had been away for years, Mary O'Brien had been a loyal customer of the Seelie Tree Apothecary since it had opened. Carissa felt comfortable making a gesture of support and even felt a little guilty that she hadn't done so earlier.

"Yes, what is it? You can ask me anything."

Through tears, Mrs. O'Brien made a request. "The doctors don't know what's wrong with my husband, even though they're trying. I've just gotten him back. I can't lose him now. You're a healer, Cari, a good one. I know you are."

Carissa understood where she was going. She squeezed her arm gently. "I'm not a doctor, Mrs. O'Brien. I'm sorry, I wouldn't know how to help with something like a coma."

"But you have magic?"

Cari's stomach turned. She wasn't skilled in magic, not enough, anyway. She opened her mouth to argue, but Mrs. O'Brien wouldn't hear it.

"Would you please, try? For me, Cari? All you have to do is look at him."

Carissa let out a frustrated breath. Finally, she said, "All right, I'll stop in sometime tomorrow, but I can't make any promises."

A hitched sigh of relief escaped Mrs. O'Brien, and she hugged Cari so tightly she thought she might lose all the air in her own lungs. Finally, the woman let go and thanked her. Carissa wasn't sure the thanks was warranted.

***

Carissa arrived home late that evening. She was surprised to be met with the scent of pecan. From the hallway, Cari saw a minuscule form zip out of the kitchen and back into it. She closed the door and walked up the foyer, through the hall, and down into the kitchen. At the end of the steps, she was met with a floating piece of pecan pie. She dodged it, but it followed closer to her mouth.

"Cynth, Hiya, stop it," she said. Her eyes found the two sprites sitting on opposite sides of Maren's shoulders from where her assistant was sitting at the kitchen table. She and Nan were both laughing as the sprites pointed to the counter. It seemed that Chaos alone was controlling the pie. She had her tiny hands out. The sparkling flow of faerie magic shot from her fingertips right to the sweet like a nearly invisible string. Her elfish eyes could hardly believe it.

The piece of pie pursued her right up to the counter, where she set down her purse.

"All right, I'll try it." She placed her hand below the slice and Chaos set it into her palm. Then she went to the cabinet, opened it, and took out a plate.

Turning to her grandmother and Maren, she said, "I thought all your trial baking was done yesterday."

"I'm trying a variety of recipes." Maren put a clear lid on the three-quarters of pie left between her and Carissa's grandmother.

Cari took a fork from the drawer and leaned against the island. She stuck it into the pecan and took a bite. It was a sugary, nutty flavor. Good, but a little overdone.

"How is it?" Maren asked.

Carissa, in the middle of a fairly dry bite, put her fingers in front of her mouth while she chewed. Chaos tugged at her sleeve. She looked down at the sprite's eager eyes.

"Chaos helped," Maren commented.

With every set of eyes in the room on her, Carissa swallowed the bite and answered.

"It's great," she said. A passing smile between her and Nan was missed by the rest of the group, except for Chaos. Fortunately, though, the faerie tilted her head and looked between them. The upraised eyebrow told Carissa that she hadn't fully understood their shared criticism of the pie. Looking closer at the sprite, she dusted her fingers off and set down her plate.

"Come here," she said, laying her palm flat for Chaos to climb onto. The sprite tilted her head the other way before reluctantly agreeing to fly into her hand. Carissa brought her to eye level.

"What is it?" Maren asked.

The sprite's wings were pitch black with almost a radiant sheen. Carissa didn't want to alarm her friend—or Chaos, for that matter—so she didn't answer directly. Instead, she lied.

"Nothing." She shared another look with Nan, who got up from her seat.

"Time for the nature faeries to scoot off to bed." Nan opened the back door and waved a reluctant trio outside. Chaos flew from Carissa's hand faster than the other two, but then stopped at the door and let Hiya and Cynth out first. Hiya didn't hesitate or even notice that Chaos was being nice, but Cynth waited the two girl faeries flew out together. It really was heartwarming to see them getting along.

"So," Maren said as Nan shut the door. "What happened after I left?"

Carissa put her hands on her face and sighed. "Mr. O'Brien was taken to a hospital. Everyone was pretty upset. Cam got it into his mind to call the mayor, who sent a squad of officers to the scene to question witnesses, and Mr. Morely demanded to see the mayor. So, Mayor Belkin told Cam that he was still in his office and Mr. Morely could come down to City Hall and see him."

"And? What happened then?"

"What do you think happened?"

Nan laughed. "I'll bet half of the Mossies followed him to spread some hysteria about the castle being haunted."

Carissa wasn't even surprised by Nan's accurate description. She put a hand on her sore neck and rubbed her tired muscles.

"That must've been something. Were they panicky?" Maren's eyes were lighting up, and Cari knew it wasn't concern but regret that she hadn't been there herself to tell all her friends about it the next day. Carissa grabbed her piece of pie to put it in the fridge, thinking about how her assistant was going to divulge anything she told her to her friends tomorrow anyway. Shutting the refrigerator, Carissa decided it best to give Maren her view of things before others put ideas into her head.

"The people all seemed convinced that it was Clancy who pushed Mr. O'Brien."

"Clancy?" Maren seemed unsure. "A three-foot nothing like that pushing a nearly six-foot man off a wall? Is that even possible?"

"I don't think so," Carissa said, "but I'm not sure. Barnaby is certain Clancy didn't do it, and he was with him the whole time."

"Well," Maren folded her arms, "he is his cousin. Of course, he would defend him."

"Clancy wouldn't do this." Nan returned to her seat. "Tell me, why do people think it was him?"

Carissa told her nan about the words "red cap" uttered by Mr. O'Brien.

Nan put a hand to her jaw, thinking. "Unless it's not referring to a hat," she mumbled. Cari heard her, but Maren spoke at the same time.

"That's a pretty damaging piece of evidence."

"Circumstantial," Cari corrected.

"Look at you with the police jargon." Maren stood. "Well, we're not going to solve it tonight. I'd better get going. Tomorrow's another workday. See you bright and early."

"See you." Carissa followed her to the door and waved as she left. She locked up behind her.

Nan stood in the hallway, arms crossed.

"What?" Carissa asked.

"Are we locking it all the time now?"

Cari realized her hand was still on the doorknob. She leaned on it rather than lifting her hand away.

"I don't know, Nan. I've just had this horrible feeling this last week." Carissa looked at the bookcase in the sitting room. Walking over to it, she reached on the top shelf and took down the small keepsake box they kept there.

Carissa took a piece of paper from the box and sat in the armchair. Nan took a place on the sofa. Cari handed her the note.

"The letter from Raven Corvus?" Nan pushed back her glasses. "You think Mr. O'Brien's fall has to do with this?"

"I think all of this has to do with it. I thought that these were just separate events, but one unseelie fae, then two, then three causing trouble in Moss Hill?" She shook her head. "I don't think it's a coincidence. This note was sent to warn us."

Nan handed the note back to her. "This wasn't all that was sent. As I recall it, the note came with a helper."

"Nan, Chaos can't help with this."

"Are you sure?" Nan's eyebrow rose in that classic look that told her she was missing something.

"She's just a little sprite."

"Though she be but little, she is—"

"Fierce," Carissa finished. Trust Nan, the librarian, to quote Shakespeare at a time like this. "I know, Nan, but I don't want her to be in any danger."

Nan left the sofa.

"It's your choice. Do what you think is best." Right at the step into the hallway, Nan turned around. "Just remember that no one who does anything worthwhile does it alone, even if they think they did. Goodnight." Her hand waved as she turned the corner.

Her grandmother had a point, and Cari intended to follow that advice. It was more than worthwhile to save Cam from suspicion or prove Clancy's innocence, and she wasn't going to solve this on her own. But, if Cari was right, there was only one person who could help. If a ghostly apparition is really was what pushed Mr. O'Brien, then what she really needed in order to stop it was a ghost.

Chapter 10
Frightful Feelings

Alden wasn't answering. Carissa gathered another bagful of the summoning powder and spread it on the counter. She kept a stockpile tucked on the last shelf at the back of the store beneath the vases she kept in the event anyone ever sent flowers, which they didn't, so it wasn't likely to be discovered. Using her elf-light, she tried one more time in the early morning, a half hour before her assistant was scheduled to arrive.

"Show thee, ankou."

She waited. Nothing happened. Her shoulders dropped. Her hands lay flat against the table as she just stood there, hoping this was just an extremely delayed response to the spell. Finally, she had to give up. She grabbed the waste bin and swooshed the herbs off the wooden surface.

A tapping at her door gave her hope for one second that it was Alden, but ankous didn't knock. Instead, it was Barnaby. The poor leprechaun looked half out of his mind. As she walked to the door and opened it, she could see that his green hat was worse for the wear.

"Are you all right, Barn?"

"May I come in?" His dark eyes welled.

"Of course." She pushed the door farther open.

He dragged his feet inside. He should have known he never needed to ask to come inside the shop and, in fact, he never had before. Even when he himself had been accused of a crime months ago, he hadn't looked this upset.

"I can't find Clarence anywhere. I've looked wherever my brain could think to, and I just don't see where he's gone to."

"Oh, Barnaby, I'm sorry. Why don't you come on back and have a seat?"

She led him to the back room, where he climbed up onto the black leather chair by the computer desk. The leprechaun was half its size. His hands were folded in his lap with the hat scrunched between them. Carissa pulled up a stool beside him.

"Did you check the winery?"

"Yes." He sniffed.

"How about the pub?" she suggested.

He nodded.

She rattled off a few other places, but he had checked them all. By the look of his bloodshot eyes, he'd been up all night doing just that.

She tried to be helpful, but she couldn't think of anything else to say except, "I'm sure he'll turn up."

"Turn up!" His volume startled her. "He very well might 'turn up,' but do you know what they'll say? They'll say he hid because he was guilty!"

"But you know he's not," Carissa stated. It wasn't a question. She believed him.

"I was there! I saw with my own eyes that he didn't push anyone."

Carissa rested her elbows on her knees. She was only a foot from Barnaby. "Did you see who did it?"

"No, but I saw who didn't do it, and that's Clancy." Barn looked right at her, the distress clear. "It's not just Clarence, it's my good name, too." He sat up straighter in his chair. "I'm not a liar."

Carissa put a hand on his shoulder. "I know you're not. I know." She patted his shoulder twice and sat back.

Barnaby glanced at her and then looked away. He cast his eyes down at the floor.

"What is it, Barn?" she asked. The leprechaun avoided her gaze.

"Barnaby?"

"I didn't lie," he said. His eyes still refused to look in her direction.

"You know something."

Now, he did look up. "I saw it, but I don't believe it myself."

"What?" she asked, leaning forward again. "Tell me what you saw."

He sighed. "I did see something right beside Clancy. It spooked me when I first got up there."

"'It?'"

"The ankou. I saw it clear as day, just sitting there beside him, and Clarence didn't see it. I tried to scream and warn him away, but it lifted a skeletal finger. Scared me to death like it was threatening me if I told." He shook his head, not quite a shudder. It was more like repulsion. "It disappeared, and Clancy nearly fell, so I grabbed him. I think it spooked him, too. He was frantic and arguing with me, but eventually, he calmed down, so I let him rest a moment. He was safely sitting on the walkway at the middle of the wall. He wasn't anywhere near Mr. O'Brien.

"Anyway, soon as he was all right I...I just had to look down. I thought maybe that the ankou had leaped off, I don't know what I was thinking. Next thing I saw a man in the air and I heard the screaming, but Clancy was right where I left him. We were at least six feet away from Cameron and O'Brien. I swear it's impossible for Clancy to have pushed him." Tears threatened to drip onto his red beard.

"Shh," Carissa held his hand, "I believe you."

"I guess," Barnaby hesitated, "I guess I have to tell the sidhe?" He glanced at her sideways. She knew what he was asking. He wanted her to do it. Barnaby didn't have the best relationship with the sidhe, most people didn't.

The sidhe were the last people she wanted to call. Still, if she didn't do it, Barnaby would have to—it would be against fae rules not to tell the people of Vale in all matters otherworldly and supernatural. She really had no choice. Well, she did have some choice.

"I'll tell the fae," she assured him. She didn't specify which ones.

"Thank you!" He shook her hand. Then he hopped off the chair and placed his cap on his head. Wrinkled as it was, it looked somewhat ridiculous, but at least he was in better spirits. "I owe you, Carissa Shae. I won't forget it," he said as he walked out of the back room and out of the store.

She sat there a moment, thinking to herself. If her parents were home, she could have gone to her father for advice. The elf historian might have had a way to help her without the sidhe getting involved, but he and her mother wouldn't return from their trip for another month. If she told the Elven Council, they'd probably tell the sidhe. If the sidhe were involved, they'd probably invoke some kind of spell to get rid of the ankou, which meant Alden would be vanquished to some kind of oblivion. She couldn't let that happen.

Of course, she was avoiding the possibility that Alden actually was guilty. Several eyewitnesses had seen a skeletal figure, and she knew he'd been on the grounds at least once before, but the ankou didn't wear a red cap.... Unless he'd possessed Clancy and made him push O'Brien? No, that didn't seem like something Alden would do. She didn't know him as well as Cam, but it just didn't fit with what she knew of him. She didn't even know if ankous could possess people.

There had to be another explanation. She didn't trust the sidhe to find it. There was one sidhe who might not *vanquish now and ask questions later*. She considered asking Varick of Vale, but thought better of it. He was bound to the rules of the Sidhe Council. It would be better to ask the elves.

The door opened and Maren stepped through, undoing her scarf as she entered. She didn't bat an eye seeing Carissa sitting there in angst. That meant something was on her mind that negated her ability to see that Cari was out of sorts.

"You will never guess what was on *Mossie Musings* today. Luckily, I couldn't sleep after hearing about your near brush of death you at Fairfield yesterday." Maren sat in the chair previously occupied by Barnaby and pulled up Tilly's blog on her computer. Carissa moved the stool closer. Clicking on the first article at the top, Maren rolled the chair out of the way so they could both read the screen.

"'Catastrophe at Fairfield Castle?'" Carissa read.

"It tells everything, and I mean everything." Maren scrolled down and read, "*Several Mossies were quick to point fingers. One victim of the mass hysteria was Cameron Larke, assistant to the mayor, who also acts as a liaison between Moss Hill and the people of Vale. When asked about his suspicions, Parker Greer, owner of the Failte Hotel, stated he had seen the two arguing earlier and overheard Mr. Larke making threats. The use of threatening language could not be corroborated with other witnesses.*"

Maren looked at Carissa, whose eyes were glued to the screen. "She doesn't seem to be taking Parker's side," Maren said. "She says later in the article that the only witness against him is Parker, and she brings up the fact that they were vying for the same job at one point. Anyone who knew Parker would know that he's just the kind to make things up like that."

Carissa heard her but wasn't reassured. A tiny part of her might have been put at ease knowing that Maren had no illusions about Parker. She'd nearly forgotten about the hand-holding after dinner the night of committee planning. That was one less argument she had to have with a friend.

Carissa kept reading out loud so that Maren wouldn't think she was completely ignoring her. "*Several eyewitnesses reported seeing a ghost on the castle grounds that night. Some describe the being as a skeletal specter, some as a short, burly man with long teeth and talon-like fingers in a red cap. Others are quick to point out that the red cap is a signature look of one of the town's most notorious residents, a clurichaun named Clarence, known for his excessive drinking."* She stopped a moment, both to catch her breath and to mentally process what she'd read.

"Yes, she points to Clancy as a suspect, but," Maren scrolled to the end of the article, "here, it says: *'In a frightening situation like this, thoughts and feelings are often overwhelmed. Fact, fiction, and fantasy have a tendency to mix together, as is one logical explanation for the incongruous witness testimonies. How does one determine the truth? Keep calm, Mossies, and keep in mind that the possibilities range from accident to any number of accusations, but the truth is likely somewhere in between.'"*

Maren left Carissa there reading for a while. She didn't want to miss a word, from the accusations against Cam to the mention of Mr. O'Brien's utterance of the words "red cap." She could vaguely hear Maren greeting their first customer when she finished the passage.

Once the words sank in, Carissa sprang to the coat rack and took out her phone, dialing furiously. Cam answered on the first ring.

"I need you to meet me after work today, bring the car and leave the driver."

"Vale? Carissa, the mayor doesn't want—"

"It doesn't matter what the mayor wants. We need to prove your innocence and Clancy's, too." She hung up before he could argue any further.

Chapter 11
Ruins and Red Fae

Fairfield Castle was visible on the way to Mount Vale. Carissa's attention drifted out the car window as she and Cameron traveled in silence. Both were too preoccupied with worry and not seeing eye to eye on how to solve the present crisis.

"I think it's a mistake," Cam finally said. He kept his eyes glued to the dirt path ahead.

"You wanted to go to Vale two weeks ago."

Cam's eyes nearly popped out of his head. "To invite the fae to the All Hallows' Eve celebration. Not to talk to them about a fae attempting to murder a Mossie." He took a sharp breath. "The minute the case is handed over to the fae, we'll lose control of the castle entirely and the investigation."

"You're sounding more and more like the mayor."

Cam pulled his eyes away from the road long enough to glance at her. "Why shouldn't I? Mayor Belkin's done a lot for Moss Hill. I don't see anything wrong with being more like him."

"You said yourself that the team Belkin sent saw suspicious activity today too."

"Some rocks fell, just like they did with Mrs. Alcott. It's not a big deal; it's a construction site."

"But they had already cleared the debris."

"From the areas overlooking the courtyard. Today, they traveled to the parts that are still in ruins. Of course, they encountered some danger. It doesn't mean there are ghosts or fae or anything there." His tone became more argumentative as his knuckles grew whiter around the steering wheel.

"Besides," he added, "you said you didn't want to involve the sidhe because Alden was there a few days ago and the sidhe aren't exactly friendly with ankous."

Carissa turned toward the window, staring at the castle. Part of her hoped for a sign that their deceased friend was still there. "He isn't answering my summoning spells," she said softly.

Cam looked between her and the road. "How many times have you tried?"

"I've been trying all day."

"Well, maybe he's busy."

"Busy doing what, exactly? What would an ankou be doing all day that he can't answer when magically called on?"

Carissa didn't look to see Cam's reaction this time but kept her eyes on the castle. It was a good thing she did, too, because the next second she saw something like a flash of light coming from the castle's direction. She sat up, bringing her eyes closer to the glass. Another flash meant it wasn't just her imagination.

"Did you see that?" she asked.

"See what?"

"Steer right. Turn onto Fairfield Drive."

"We missed that turn-off a while back."

"It's close enough. The ground is just grass, veer right," she stressed.

He did so, but not without an argument. "Now we're going in by ourselves? I hate to point this out, but your plans are becoming less and less logical."

"I saw something."

The tires screeched to a halt. Cari's seat belt grabbed her and yanked her back against the cushion.

Cam faced her with a wordless exasperation. Then he put the car in reverse and started to travel backward down the drive.

"What happened to '*it's just construction*?'" Cari challenged.

He stopped and put the car in park. He stared at the castle a good while, thinking. He had to know she was right. If he thought O'Brien's fall was an accident, then there would be no harm in them going to Fairfield. If he thought it was a fae, then they should continue to Vale as Cari had suggested.

"It could be a human, a trespasser," Cam brought up a third option.

"Doing what? Rigging loose stones to give way on the walls?"

"I don't know, maybe."

"If it is a human, I think I can handle that," Cari said. "I've faced a hobgoblin before, a human should be easy. Unless it's a druid, in which case, onward to Vale." She sat with her arms folded, waiting for his answer.

He put the car in drive and slowly headed toward the castle. "I'm going on the record to say I don't like this."

"What does that even mean—on the record? This is not City Hall. There is no record, Cam. Just you and me and maybe, if we're lucky, Alden."

"You think it was him you saw?"

"I don't know. There's only one way to find out." The car stopped, and she opened the door. So did Cam.

They walked through the gate gingerly, looking in all directions. They saw nothing all the way to the end of the courtyard until they arrived at the main castle building.

"Wait. I'll go first." Cam swallowed his fear and stepped up to the lead. At the top of the stairs, they saw another flash and then a shadow moving.

"Something's there," Cam whispered hoarsely.

The shadow seemed to stop as if it heard them. The two, both at the top of the steps now, watched as the shadow turned toward them. It lingered in that position long enough that Cari thought time had stood still.

Carissa tried to move but Cam's arm flung out in front of her, keeping her back. The shadow grew.

"Hello?" a meek voice said. "Is someone there?"

That was definitely the voice of a living person. Not only that, but Cari was sure she'd heard the person before. She pushed Cameron's hand down and brushed past him. He followed quickly behind her.

"You!" Cari said the moment she saw the tourist with his camera in his hands, standing at the top of the ramparts.

His brow hovered above his glasses. "You? Should I be concerned that you're following me around?"

Cari felt her cheeks redden. She couldn't very well admit that she had been eavesdropping the other night. But he was poking his nose around Moss Hill, and she wasn't going to back down from telling him that that was unacceptable.

Cameron stepped beside her. "Following him?"

Cari ignored his question. "What are you doing up here? Don't you know you're trespassing?"

Reginald held the camera up and snapped a picture of Cari and Cam. "It's public property." He looked down at the camera, pressing some buttons on the screen.

"Public to Mossies," she corrected. Even that wasn't certain since O'Brien was contesting the town's claim to it, but she wasn't going to get into that with him.

Reginald tilted his head to the side. "I don't think that's how that works."

Cam laughed—his tactic to diffuse the tension in uncomfortable situations. He walked past Cari and extended a hand to the stranger. "You're right, under normal circumstances, but there was an accident here the other day, so my friend is a little jumpy," he said. "I'm Cameron Larke. It looks like you know Carissa Shae."

The man locked hands and nodded in Cari's direction. "We've met before. Reginald Smith. My friends call me Reg."

Cam, still hand in hand with Reginald, gave Cari a proud grin, like this proved he was right about there being nothing supernatural here.

"Well, Reg, as I was saying, normally the castle is open to the public, but it's been under construction, and there was an accident here the other night."

"Accident?" Reginald scoffed, he looked Cam up and down. "Larke, right, the one arguing with him that night? Don't worry, I don't believe you did it, but I don't for a second think that it was an accident." Reg pushed his glasses up and scrolled through the camera. Then, finding whatever he was looking for, he took the camera off his neck and handed it to them. Cameron took it reluctantly.

"What are we looking at?" Cam held the screen between them. Cari could only make out a blur on a background of stone.

"That is what attempted to murder your Mr. O'Brien."

Carissa noted the date on the camera. It was not taken today. "You've been here before."

Reg took the camera back, slinging it around his neck. "True. That morning you all were here. I might've introduced myself, but you all got spooked and left right after. You understand why I didn't make an introduction." Despite his statement, Reg explained, "I thought you might think I threw the stones. Anyway, I didn't see anything at the time, but then I caught this on a picture."

"I don't know what you caught on camera, but it doesn't look like a ghost to me," Cam said.

"It's not a ghost, it's a fae."

Carissa's eyes widened. She gripped Cameron's arm. "A redcap. When I saw you in the woods the other day, you mentioned that specifically as a type of faerie."

Reg's smile was all smug vindication. "Based on the accounts of several Mossie witnesses, it was either a Grim Reaper or a redcap."

Cam's mouth dropped the more Reg mentioned faeries. Cari understood. She'd had the same reaction almost every time she'd seen this tourist.

Cameron eventually snapped out of it. "Faeries? What? That's not possible."

He looked between Carissa and Reg. Cari looked down at the floor. She didn't really see the point in denying Reginald's claims anymore, not with what Tilly had been posting on her blog. Cam's gasp meant he interpreted her silence differently.

"No," he said, "you can't both think it was Clancy? Just because he was wearing a red hat—"

"I don't know who Clancy is," Reg butted into Cam's revelation, "but I doubt the redcap has a cute name like that."

The thin man crossed his arms and spread his stance, filling his chest with false importance. "A redcap is a vengeful dark faerie who wears a red hat and loves castles. More specifically, he loves the battles that happen inside them. He is said to have died in war, and he thrives on the terror of it."

Reg sliced the air with his hand. "He'll attack anyone without reason. The scariest part? His cap wasn't always red. It turns redder with every victim."

"Okaaay." Cam took a step back. "Thank you for that information. I will mention that to the mayor, but right now I'm afraid you'll have to leave."

"No problem." The man pushed back his glasses again. "I was done anyway. Though I do have to say, for a town that's so closely connected to the Otherworld, the people here don't seem to know that much about it."

Cam laughed, but his nervousness made it come out higher pitched than probably intended. "I don't know what you're talking about."

"If you say so." The man took a step forward.

"Can we give you a ride somewhere?" Carissa offered. Cam turned around and gave her the large eyes that universally meant *What are you doing?* What she was doing was trying to keep an eye on this nosy sneak.

"No, I rented a bicycle. I saw that some of the locals prefer for transportation around the island." He smiled.

Was he showing off his knowledge of Mossies? Did he smile like that because he knew Cari was one of the ones who bicycled around town? Whatever his reasons, the expression was creepy.

He walked past them to leave. Cari gave him ample space to pass. Once the tourist was gone, Cam spun around. He waved his hands, pointing at the stairs with open palms.

"What?" Carissa asked.

"I think we found our ghost." Cam put the word *ghost* in air quotes. "Think about it. He was here the day the stones fell on Mrs. Alcott, he might've been here the night Mr. O'Brien fell."

"You're saying he pushed him?"

"Or threw a stone at him or scared him, or maybe he didn't cause the fall, but he was definitely strange. You have to admit that."

"It doesn't change the fact that people reported seeing the ankou or the redcap."

"You believe him?"

"I don't know. He's been getting a lot of information from Tilly's website about things we shouldn't really be telling non-Mossies. One of us has to talk to her about that. Still, he might be right about the redcap. It'd be easy enough to prove."

"The fae archives?"

Carissa nodded.

"All right. Let's get out of here and take a look at what the archives have. It's a better plan than going to the fae anyway."

"Oh, we are still going to Vale. You drive. I'll look up the redcap on my phone."

Cam frowned. "Sometimes I hate technology."

The moment they took their first step down the stairs, Cari pulled out her smartphone, knowing that the closer they got to Vale, the worse reception she'd receive. The phone was slow and the word "redcap" didn't pull up anything.

In the courtyard, Cam's arm went out in front of Cari. She and Cam stopped. There was a shadow, just like the first time she'd come here. It was less visible and more like movement that they could only catch out of the corners of their eyes.

"Reginald?" Cam asked loudly, standing tall. He shrank a bit. "Alden?" He asked in a quieter tone. Then, in a softer, much shakier voice, he asked, "Redcap?" The shadow moved again. Cam grabbed Cari's arm and raced the wind to the gate.

They were past the outer wall and to the car before Cameron let go of her hand.

"Cam, calm down."

"I am calm," he shouted as he clicked the door. They both sat inside.

Carissa held the phone up to show him the title of the entry she'd just found.

He reached for the phone and drew it closer to his bewildered eyes: "The Redcap: A Castle Menace."

The problem was, it wasn't in the Moss Hill Fae Archives. It was on Tilly's blog.

Chapter 12

Toil and Trouble

"How awful!" Hela exclaimed. The head elf's daughter, newly married and visiting her parents with her new husband, Fen, sat beside Carissa and Cameron in her parents' backyard. The blooming garden paled in comparison to Hela's dress. Her red hair was more vibrant than Carissa's and fell against her embroidered gold neckline with a radiant sheen. Her peach dress shimmered in the sun. Her husband's long, blond hair had almost the same brilliance. His azure eyes questioned her as he took a croissant from the tray that Sal, the elfkin helper, had brought out for afternoon tea.

"Is Mr. O'Brien expected to recover?"

"The doctors don't know exactly why he's in a coma. Without understanding the cause, there's no way to know how to cure him," Cam answered.

Sal poured the tea and Cam immediately went for his. "Careful," Sal said, "that's—"

Cam pulled the cup away, putting a hand to his burned mouth and spilling the tea. The liquid burned his fingers now, too, and he dropped the cup onto its saucer, shaking his hand to soothe the pain.

"...Hot," Sal finished. The elfkin put a napkin down on the table, blotting the spilled tea.

"Sorry."

Sal, never one to chide another person, said, "Think nothing of it."

Carissa placed one hand to Cam's chin and one on his hand. She used her elf-light to heal him. This seemed to spark an idea in Hela.

She touched her husband's arm. "We should send an elf healer to see what we can do."

Carissa let go of him and took a croissant. Cam's eyes remained on Cari long enough to make her to blush. She looked up to see Hela with a cheeky grin that only deepened the redness of her face.

Cam cleared his throat. "That would be great."

Sal put the tray down and scratched his head. Being an elfkin, he did not have the authority to sit with them for tea, but he spoke his mind freely among the group.

"So you believe that there's something on the castle grounds? A ghost?"

"Not a ghost, a redcap." Cari wished she could show the entry from the fae archives, or rather from Tilly's blog, but her technology wouldn't work in Vale. The Otherworld didn't carry signals from the human world, and there weren't any cell towers nearby to transmit those signals anyway. The fae wouldn't even consider it, given their belief that certain technologies were harmful to nature.

By now, Master Rolin, the head elf, was coming down the steps to the garden patio. Beside him walked his wife, Marquette, in an elegant dress like her daughter's. Briefly, Cari wondered what it would be like to be so fancy every day. As beautiful as their wardrobes were, Carissa had a feeling she would get tired of formal wear pretty quickly. Rolin's timing was impeccable, as he caught the last words Cari had uttered.

"The redcap? What is it you could possibly be speaking of?" he asked.

Cari and Cam stood. Hela embraced her parents. Fen left his seat and lowered his head in deference to the master and mistress of the house, his in-laws. Sal bowed, which caused Cam to awkwardly do the same. Even a month into his position, he hadn't fully grasped how to act in front of the head elf. Cari wondered how he would do in front of the Sidhe Council if they ever called on him. Lucky for Cam, they never would agree to talk to a human.

Carissa nodded as Fen had done and then answered Rolin's question. "Sir, the redcap is a dark fae—"

"I'm aware of what the redcap is, I wonder why you are speaking of it." Rolin sat as Sal pulled out the chair. He flung his robe to the side and Sal poured his tea. He and his wife added a stately aura to the table.

"Sir, we believe the redcap has taken up residence in Fairfield Castle," Carissa said.

Rolin brought his cup to his lips and stopped, holding the tea in midair. He set the cup back down. Outwardly, he appeared to have resumed his calm, if he'd ever lost it, but Cari sensed Rolin was more deeply troubled by the news than he let on.

"The unseelie fae," he said, referring to the evil-natured faeries, "left this island long ago and agreed never to return. The redcap was among the first to leave. The castle was in peace. Peace was too dull for him. He wanted to go. I doubt he would return."

"Well," Cam said, looking fairly pleased with himself, "there is the possibility that it's a human pretending to be a fae."

Carissa shot Cam a glare that might have been as frightening as the redcap himself. Then she made her plea to Rolin.

"Many witnesses have reported seeing it. I would like to request—" Mid-sentence, she realized Cam had actually done her a favor. His doubt and Rolin's could be used to avoid the one thing she feared. "Since there's doubt, I don't think the sidhe need to be involved. I'd like to request the elves look into the matter."

"The elves only serve Vale," Rolin said, taking a sip from his cup.

Hela, who couldn't possibly understand Cari's hesitation to involve the sidhe, backed her friend anyway. "Father, I'm sure you could spare a few elves for a few hours."

Rolin sat stoically. He and Carissa stared at one another like it was a contest. Finally, Rolin smiled at his daughter. "I would like to help your friend, but if it is the redcap, I'm afraid the elves will not be able to help."

"Surely, you're as strong as—"

"It's not a matter of strength," the head elf interrupted. "It's a matter of how to vanquish a powrie with as much power as the redcap. This is not a fae, not technically. It's more like a ghost, the ghost of a fallen soldier. The redcap was a half-fae who fell in battle. It's a half-living thing. It will require more than fae magic to get rid of this spirit creature."

"What more?" Cam asked.

"The castle grounds must be cleansed," Rolin paused, "by a priest."

Cam's eyebrows knitted together. "Like an exorcism?"

Carissa stared at the table. "That would vanquish any spirits on the premises, including an ankou."

Rolin raised an eyebrow. The head elf must've known that the ankou had been instrumental against the hobgoblin that had attacked Carissa months back, but he may not have realized that she cared for him as a friend. Even so, no fae was fond of ghosts and spirits—especially not the ankou.

"Places that are sacred to our shared history should be cleansed. I'll ensure that we send guards to help in the mission. Moss Hill can provide the priest." Rolin set his eyes on the tea and croissants as if the conversation were over.

"How is the castle sacred to our history?" Cari asked.

"It's where we took a stand against the unseelie and drove off the dark faeries from our land." He picked up the teacup and brought it to his lips.

"Our land…" Carissa's heart tingled as she asked, "is it Hy Brasil?"

The teacup clanged onto the saucer. Cari and Cam both jumped. It was an unexpected display of anger from the head of elves.

"Where did you hear that name?"

"I, uh, I overheard some people talking, that's all," she said. She feared to be more specific. She even feared for Reginald given Rolin's furious expression.

"Some questions are better left unasked," he said. This time, he drank his tea and turned his head away from them to make it clear that the conversation was done.

Cam stood. "Well, we appreciate all the information and your help with the, uh, castle." He bowed to Rolin. "The tea was lovely," he said to Sal. He faced the Lady Marquette, as well as Hela and Fen. "And, of course, the company was delightful." He held a hand out to Carissa, who had to go along with this nervous display by smiling and exiting with him. Once her back was turned, she rolled her eyes at Cam, showing her displeasure at his hasty, nervous exit. Sal showed them out.

"Dreadful," the elfkin said as they walked. "You know, Cari, I don't have much elf-magic in me, but if you need anything from me, I'm here."

They stopped in the doorway and Cam put a hand to his neck. "Actually, there is. I came all this way and I, uh," Cam clapped against his suit pockets, searching for something. Finally, he found a gold envelope. It was intricately designed and addressed to the Elven Council. "I forgot to give this to master, uh, Head Elf Rolin."

He clutched it with both hands. Then, he turned to Cari. "Do you think I should go back?"

"Don't you fret," Sal said. "I'll present it to the master when his mood lightens."

Cari wasn't sure his mood ever lightened, but she reached up to give Sal a kiss on the cheek. "Thank you, Sal."

"Yes, thank you!" Cam beamed.

Cari was grateful to Sal for his help with Cam's dilemma, but with the matter of the redcap, there was nothing the elfkin could do. Cameron and Carissa walked to the car in silence. The moment grew heavier with each step.

Cari turned her locket and shifted them out of the Otherworld. The car became visible, and they sat inside. Turning on the car and reversing, Cameron sighed as he shifted gears and they sped down the road.

"I'll tell the mayor about the priest."

"Not yet," Cari argued. "Not until we figure out a way to keep Alden safe."

"We don't even know if he's there."

Carissa scoffed. "He's a friend, Cam."

"Yes, he's a friend. He's also passed on. If he's there on the grounds when the priest does his cleansing, maybe he'll get to rest in peace. Doesn't he deserve that?"

"You don't know if that will happen."

"How can it not? Alden was a good person in life, he's a good person in death. If he's banished from here, where do you think he'll go? This might be best for him."

"You're guessing. You'd honestly leave Alden's fate up to a guess?"

He took a breath and exhaled wearily. "Then what do you suggest?"

Carissa put a hand on his shoulder. "I think we should go to Macara."

"The Morrigan's sister? No offense, but she's odd. She avoids everyone in town, and the few people who have talked to her say she's a lot like her sister. Not mean but blunt. She criticizes everyone."

Carissa laughed. "So you don't want to go see her because she's blunt and you're afraid she might criticize you?"

Cam grunted. "I didn't say I wasn't going there. But how do you know you can trust her? I mean, how do you even know she can help?"

Cari's smile faded, recalling Macara's sister. Her eyes drifted back out the window. "She and Miss Morgan both helped me before, each in their own way." She opened the window, not caring how cold it was. She needed some air.

Thinking about Macara and her sister reminded her of the first moment she realized Miss Morgan was more than she seemed. The day she'd received the note warning of danger in Moss Hill, it was Miss Morgan who had understood the message.

"I think when this is over, we should tell the sidhe about the note," Carissa said.

"What note?" Cam asked.

"The one from Ms. Corvus. The one that came with Chaos."

Cam's eyes flashed with recognition. "To tell them that 'dangerous fae' were coming? That'll make them change their minds about the tourism."

"It's better than allowing this invasion and letting more people die."

"Who said anything about an invasion?" Cam's pitch rose and the car jostled as he drove too quickly down the road.

Cari listed off the threats they'd already encountered: "A ban sidhe, a leanansidhe, a hobgoblin, and now the redcap. That's more unseelie in the last few months than we've seen in the last two hundred years."

"*If* there's a redcap."

Carissa looked at him incredulously. "Are we really going to start that again?"

Cam clamped his jaw and focused on the road. Carissa looked out the window, steaming about how obstinate Cam was being. She didn't want to blame him, but he was being more of an obstacle than a help by trying to keep the mayor's agenda. *With him acting like this, Tilly is welcome to him.* Carissa rolled her eyes at herself. On top of everything, she didn't need thoughts like that constantly popping into her head. That, she decided, was Cameron's fault, too.

Chapter 13

Druids and Dread

Macara was no longer staying at the Everly residence. Carissa had thought her lack of presence at the dinner party was strange. Apparently, Macara found it better to be a recluse. According to Cam, she lived in a house further up the side of Mount Ashling. It was a cottage, really. The whole of it would barely stretch across the Everly's living room. Even Miss Morgan had chosen to stay with the Everlys rather than live in a place like this.

Cameron pulled into the driveway, which was long as the mountain zig-zagged so as to make access to homes more challenging. As they pulled up, Cari began to see the charm of the place. For its lack of size, the home found its appeal in a myriad of other quirks. Sturdy, cinnamon-red bricks, dark, moss-green bearings on the Tudor-style, tiled roof, and a brilliant, candy-apple door greeted them. Quaint was the word for it. It was hardly what Carissa expected as a residence for a woman who was once hailed as part of a triple-goddess figurehead.

Cari and Cam stepped out of the car. Before she even closed the door, Carissa felt a strong current chill her to the bone as the wind came in from the ocean. At nearly seven in the evening the sun was still up, but the temperature was dropping. The warmth of the indoors could be felt radiating through a side window. The green curtains were drawn, but Carissa could see an orange glow behind them.

Cam knocked. No butler answered. No one answered, in fact, but the door creaked open, and a pleasant voice called out, "Well, come in, you two, before you catch a cold."

Cameron led the way, though Cari knew he would have preferred to follow. The scene inside was more luxurious than Carissa had expected. Greeted with the scent of sage, they entered a rustic kitchen complete with dark wood counters and matching beams overhead. The roar of a crackling fire drew Cari's attention to the next room where a rust-colored sofa and armchair lay on hardwood floors in front of a cozy fireplace. The décor consisted of ferns, mistletoe, celosia, and herbs scattered around the home.

The concoction on the stove reminded Carissa that she and Cam had not had dinner. Macara seemed to sense this. She turned from the pot, ladle in hand, and pointed to the cabinets.

"Bowls are on top to the right, spoons below. I hope you're in the mood for butternut squash soup." The tall woman with long raven-black hair turned her back to them again, stirring the soup until it was ready.

Cameron did not need to be told twice. He walked to the cabinet and took out the bowls. Cari grabbed some cloth napkins she saw sitting on the counter—three of them. *Had Macara known they would visit?* A trivet sat on the table, awaiting the cauldron, which Macara lifted with potholders and set down between them. The three grabbed their servings and sat.

"Thank you," Carissa said.

"It smells heavenly." Cam breathed the aroma in with eyes closed.

"You're very welcome." Macara took a spoonful and let out a satisfied sigh.

"We missed you at the Everlys' dinner," Carissa said. It was her polite way of getting information. Macara's smile indicated she knew that Cari was prying. Carissa was a Mossie, after all, and it was a curious thing that such a close friend of the family would not attend such an important dinner party.

"I'm sure I missed MacLir asking about all those stories of old times. He always asks the same questions. The ego on that man." She took a dismissive sip of soup and sat back in her chair. "Now, tell me what brought you here."

Carissa was still trying to wrap her brain around Macara's definition of 'old times.' The only story told at dinner was of the Everlys' ancestor, Cormac MacAirt, which had to have been hundreds of years ago. Macara might very well be that old, but it was difficult to imagine. And what did that have to do with MacLir's ego?

Realizing that Macara was waiting for a response, Carissa set down her spoon and fiddled with the napkin on her lap.

"You've heard about Mr. O'Brien?" she ventured.

"Yes." Macara held her face still, slightly tilted, waiting for her to continue.

"I'm sure you also know that there are several suspects implicated in the accident," Cari said.

Cam moved his spoon about the bowl, absentmindedly stirring as Cari continued.

"We think it might be a redcap."

"Or the ankou?" Macara added. Her tone wasn't accusing, but Cam took it that way.

"Not Alden." Cam shook his head, adamantly refuting the possibility.

"Alden is missing," Carissa clarified. "I'm worried that he might still be on the grounds." She explained what Rolin had told her about how to cast the redcap away. "We don't know what will happen if a priest does a cleansing. He might banish Alden, and we're concerned about what that would mean."

Macara took another sip of soup and paused to bring the napkin to her mouth. Cam exchanged a look with Cari. She tried to be polite and wait out a response. The suspense was torturous.

The wheels were turning in Macara's mind; Cari could see it in her charcoal eyes. *Have they always been this unearthly color?* Her steely features settled on a word.

"Jane." Macara lifted her spoon again. "Jane is your answer." Then she brought the soup to her mouth and continued her supper.

"How is Jane the answer?" Cam asked.

Macara smiled. There was something hidden behind her eyes, though. "She's the sister to the current ankou. Their shared bloodline might be enough for her to summon him—if she's willing to perform a spell to do it. Once they are together in the same place, she can ground him. If he's grounded to a living person, he won't disappear—no matter what spell is cast."

Carissa looked at Cam. "Alden said that before. He grounded himself to you."

Cam squinted. "Maybe that's why he disappeared? He wasn't grounded to anyone for a while?"

"Possibly," Macara said.

"Can't he just do it again?"

"He's not here, and you can't do the spell. I could try it, though," Cari offered.

They both looked at Macara questioningly.

"Jane has the strongest connection to Alden. It has to be her."

Carissa wasn't sure that was strictly true, but if Macara was anything like her sister, she must've had her reasons for insisting that it be Jane. The only problem was that Jane had only as much fae blood as Cam, as far as Carissa was aware.

"You'll still need someone to do the spell."

"Jane can do the spell," Macara said as if it were no large matter. Carissa and Cam, however, sat stunned by the revelation that Jane had magic.

"Alden needs to be grounded to stay in this world. Any spirit does. This can be something as simple as unfinished business or as strong as an attachment to a person. For an ankou, the grounding is their mission to guide the recently dead. They can travel between the world beyond and here because their mission is strong enough to pull them back. Since Alden is missing, it's likely he's in the world beyond. If he can't come back of his own accord, he'll need someone to pull him back. That's more than a grounding. Once he's settled back in this world, there's no need to ground him further unless he's targeted. If there's no danger from a spell being directed right at him, there's no need to be grounded to a person. However, if he should be targeted specifically by magic or prayer, even a strong grounding can be broken." Macara squinted at Carissa. "Your forebears taught you nothing?"

By forebears, Macara probably meant parents. It was a question, not an accusation, but Carissa felt her cheeks burning. She picked up her spoon, trying to ignore the sting. "My parents were away a lot. My father taught me some…magic. Ironic, I know, the elf historian's daughter." She shrugged and let the words drift into the air.

She could feel Cam's sympathetic gaze on her and Macara's judgmental eyes. So, she concentrated on her bowl of soup. The sage-rich squash was mouth-wateringly creamy. It made for a good distraction.

But Macara didn't let the subject rest for long. "There's something else, I think, you wanted to ask me."

Carissa blinked a few times. *Something else? Oh, yes, the note.* "I received a note a while back from a woman named Raven Corvus."

Macara laughed. She held the napkin to her lips and stifled further cackles. "Raven Corvus? She thinks she's clever. What an obvious name!" Macara noticed Cari's open-mouthed stare. "Oh, don't mind it—do continue."

"Um, well, it warned that dark fae, the unseelie, were coming to Moss Hill."

Macara nodded. "Yes, she would have sent the note around the same time she sent one to me."

"She sent you one?" Cam asked.

"I knew she'd have sent one, yes."

"That's great!" Cam's enthusiasm made Cari flinch and give a chiding wince in his direction. He noticed. "Not about the hobgoblin, or the dark fae, of course, I mean that you knew about the note." He turned to Cari. "That means you don't have to tell the sidhe about yours." To Macara, he said, "If the sidhe needed to know about it, you probably told them, right?"

Macara put a hand to her chin and rested her eyes on Cameron. Cam squirmed in his chair.

She dropped her hand and said to Carissa, "I suppose there's no way around it. You still have to tell the sidhe. I warned them there was danger in Moss Hill two months ago and maybe more to come. You need to warn them that there's been danger for the last four months and more is *definitely* to come. They need to be prepared."

Carissa swallowed the last bite of soup. She could feel it sliding down to the pit of her stomach, along with her courage.

"They will not be pleased that you didn't show them the message right away, but they will appreciate that you're showing it to them now," Macara said.

"Well," Cam said, "thank you for the soup. I guess it's down the road to Jane's."

"They're not at home," Macara informed. "They went to visit Mr. O'Brien at the hospital. You should find what you need there." Either Cari had imagined the charcoal grey in Macara's eyes before, or she imagined the warm amber in them now. She almost thought they were reflecting the yellow-orange glow of the soup.

Cam rose to leave. Carissa stood, too, picking up her dinnerware.

"Leave it," Macara ordered.

Cari could no longer feel anything in her hands. She looked at her empty palms, thinking she had set it down. It was gone from the table entirely. She looked at Cameron, but he hadn't even noticed. He and Macara were already walking to the door. Cari whisked around, dumbfounded, peering at the sink and counters. The bowls were nowhere in sight.

It took a second for her to compose herself. She'd seen magic, plenty of it, but that was master-level. Her own skills were rudimentary in comparison. She chortled to herself. Her skills were rudimentary compared to a lot of elves if she was honest about it. She dismissed the thought and made her way to the door.

On the way out, she was stopped when Macara and Cam halted in the doorway.

Macara grabbed Cameron's arm. Carissa could only see half his face, but his eyes grew as wide as when he'd first seen the specter of Alden. The woman whispered something in his ear, which seemed to calm him. He slowly looked at Carissa, his expression heavy.

Cari wished she'd heard what Macara had said. She asked Cam after they were back in the car.

"I'm sorry," Cameron said.

"Sorry? What was she apologizing to you for?"

"No, *I'm* sorry," he stressed his remorse. "You said I was acting like the mayor and you're right. I've been putting my ambitions in front of what's best for us—Moss Hill, I mean." He was quick to correct himself.

"Wow, Macara's magic must be strong. She seems to have done a number on you."

"Yeah," he muttered. He turned the ignition and off they went to the next stop: Moss Hill Hospital.

***

It shouldn't have been surprising to Carissa that they passed Moss Hill's star reporter in the hallway. Tilly Brier's belongings sat on a chair while she put on her sweater. Adjusting her hair and hoisting the bag onto her shoulder, she continued on her way. She might not have even noticed the two of them, except that Cam took the initiative.

"I'll talk to her," he said to Cari, then walked over to Tilly. For a second Carissa was thrown, wondering why he was going over to her. It was another second before she realized that he was talking to her about toning down the references to Vale in her online articles.

Carissa left them chatting in the lobby while she made her way to the room the receptionist had indicated was Mr. O'Brien's. One floor and three rooms later, she knocked on a door. She heard talking inside, two men, she thought.

"Come in," a familiar voice said.

Familiar, it might have been, but it wasn't anyone she had expected. Instead of Mr. Everly or any of the Everlys, Magnus MacLir sat in the armchair beside the gentleman lying in the bed. The light blue walls and pristine white floors were visible by the faint glow of a lamp beside the chair. O'Brien's unresponsive form could not have been the second voice. She began to doubt she'd heard one. It was the only hospital in Moss Hill, after all, and the walls were thin enough that she might've been hearing other patients. She took a place at the foot of the bed.

"How is he?" she asked softly.

"In need of healing," Mr. MacLir replied.

Carissa bit her lip, recalling her promise to Mrs. O'Brien. She moved to the other side of the bed so that she could see the patient clearly.

Mr. O'Brien was all skin and bones. His face was sunken, and he looked weak, especially on the respirator. He did not just look like a man who'd fallen off a building, but one that had been crushed by the weight of the world. Now she understood why Mrs. O'Brien thought only magic could save him.

She was glad Hela had volunteered to send an elf to heal him. Though having seen what Macara could do, she wondered why Macara hadn't come to heal him herself. She wasn't sure how much Mr. MacLir knew about fae magic, but she wanted to be reassuring.

Remedy and Ruins

"A specialist friend of mine will come by tomorrow to see what else can be done for him," Cari said.

"A woman named Hela and a friend of hers looked at him earlier today. They couldn't heal him."

Carissa gently touched O'Brien's hand. "Then nothing can be done."

MacLir rested an elbow on the side of the armchair, bringing his face into the light. He put a hand to his chin and his blue eyes blazed.

"Why do you value your elf-light less than others?"

Carissa stood there, trying to keep her face unresponsive while she tried to process what he was asking.

MacLir had seemed skeptical when the tourist had talked about the strangeness of the town. Yet the mayor had let him stay during the meeting with the concerned Mossies, so, for some reason, Mayor Belkin wasn't worried about him overhearing the topic of the fae. He seemed to have a magnetic effect on the people around him. *Could he be fae? Or worse, unseelie fae?* This wouldn't be the first time a dark fae had posed as a human in Moss Hill.

Carissa backed away. She was on the wrong side of the room if he really was an unseelie faerie. She tried to play it cool.

"I don't know what you mean." Cari gave a forced laugh.

Magnus's laugh was real. But it was not like an evil fae, it was mirthful, not malicious. Cari tilted her head.

"Carissa, you have everything you need to cure this man. Well, between Jane, the MacAirts, and you, you have everything you need."

He dropped his hand and sat back in the chair, motioning that she should sit in hers on the other side of the bed. Reluctantly, she took the seat.

"There's one more piece to the puzzle you might need. Jane didn't finish the story about the MacAirts. When MacAirt's children and wife were taken from him to the world beyond the living, he brought them back only by drinking from a golden cup. Among other properties, it can restore one to life. The stranger gifted Cormac MacAirt with a golden cup—as he had the branch—with a price. Keeping these items tied them to the land in which they were made."

Cari gasped. The MacAirts were tied to the world beyond. That's what he was saying. That meant that Alden hadn't become ankou for no reason. It was in his family's heritage.

MacLir leaned forward again, smiling as the look of realization spread across Carissa's face. But his story had prompted more questions than answers in her mind.

"How do you know this story? Are you related to the MacAirts somehow?"

A knock on the door interrupted them. Cameron stepped inside the room and looked between the two of them.

"I'm sorry to interrupt, but, Carissa, Tilly just told me a warrant has been issued for Clancy's arrest."

Chapter 14
Happy Hauntings

Cam couldn't get involved, but Carissa stopped by the Harbridge's on her way home. She knew Mr. Harbridge's genuine affection for the leprechaun who shared his shop meant he would tell Barnaby the news as soon as he could.

By the time she arrived home, it was late. The house was asleep, which seemed like a good idea for her, too. But it was hard to sleep with so many worries drifting around in her head. She tossed and turned, unable to find a comfortable position until, finally, she decided to quit moving altogether and let go of her thoughts. She smiled briefly at the thought of the branch at the Everly's, the one that could heal people and make them fall asleep. What she wouldn't give for that right now.

Her eyes shot open. The branch and the cup: They seemed like solutions, but solutions to what? She was already in a twilight sleep and unable to process why the branch was important. Finally, she fell fast into dreaming, and her mind brought everything together.

By the time she awoke the next morning, she knew exactly what she needed to do. She got dressed and rushed off to the store without breakfast, barely saying hello and goodbye to Nan and the sprites. She'd have to talk to Nan later about how the nature faeries had virtually taken up residence indoors.

The moment she arrived at the Seelie Tree Apothecary, she tried the summoning spell again, just in case. Unsurprisingly, Alden showed no sign of appearing. She called Jane Everly, but there was no response. She looked out the window to Barnaby's, but he didn't seem to be there either. She tried Cameron's cell phone, but he, too, wasn't answering.

Frustration made its way up to her throat, and a guttural "argh" escaped her lip. Her stomach reminded her it was empty by mimicking her grunt with a noise of its own. If she couldn't do anything at the moment, she might as well eat breakfast. By its start, this was promising to be a long day. She walked next door to Gooseberry's.

The bakery worker was surprised to see a customer this early. She was still setting out items on the morning buffet. The moment Cari walked in, the girl's mouth dropped open and she lost handle of the pan. It dropped into place on the buffet, but not before the girl's thumb touched the hotplate. She pulled away sharply, waving her thumb to shake off the pain.

"Sorry." Carissa cringed. "Run it under the water."

The girl waved it off, "No, it's okay, I barely touched it."

Cari noted no noise from the kitchen and no one else around.

"Looks like your usual baker hasn't arrived yet."

"She's not coming in. Just me this morning. What can I get you?"

Carissa looked at the buffet; it was a meager offering compared to the usual, but there was fresh cornbread, cinnamon-infused by the aroma, so Cari ordered one. The girl put a substantial piece into a clear to-go container, and Cari paid, planning to eat it next door. The plan fell through when she heard a sound two tables away.

The girl disappeared to the kitchen, finishing the morning preparations. She'd said she was alone and Cari hadn't noticed any customers coming inside, but she had definitely heard someone clearing their throat.

She stopped, holding the cornbread with her elfish ears piqued, listening for the sound again. This time, she heard nothing but saw a piece of cornbread on the buffet moving. It slid two centimeters, then tumbled behind the counter.

Carissa peered over but couldn't see since the buffet was shielded. Briefly, Cari glanced toward the kitchen, but there was no sign that the worker was coming back. She walked behind the counter to see the cornbread, half eaten, hovering in midair. A second later, it fell to the floor.

There was that noise again, like someone clearing their throat. Carissa uttered the elvish phrase that allowed her to see in both worlds. There was Clancy, gripping his red hat, looking frantically around for what to do. He bolted, gripping the counter to try to hop over it, but Cari turned the locket as he struggled to get his bearings beside the register. He was about to hop off, but Carissa was already in the Otherworld and ready to catch him.

"Gotcha," she said.

She caught him midleap and pulled him back.

"Let me go!" his gruff voice demanded.

"Calm down, Clarence, I'm trying to help."

"Then let go!"

Clarissa felt him using his clurichaun magic to try to vanish, but she used her elf-light to send a zap through her fingertips onto his chest. He wheezed. It couldn't be a good feeling—like having one's breath knocked out of them.

"Will you stay put if I let go?" Cari asked.

He nodded.

"Sorry," Carissa patted his back gently.

"Some help." He grunted when he caught his breath again. His face was red, but Cari didn't think her elf-magic was solely responsible for that.

"Been hitting the bottle again?"

He glared.

"You're lucky I caught you instead of the police. Did you know Mayor Belkin has a warrant out for your arrest?"

"Why do you think I'm here? Think I like stealing human food from a second-rate bakery?"

So many things were wrong with that statement. "I think you love stealing, you do it enough at the winery from what Barnaby says. Does he know you're here?"

He scoffed. "That bully. I got an earful from him the night of the accident, and I've no mind to hear another earful today." He put on his hat and pushed past Carissa.

"Where do you think you're going?"

"Anywhere but here." He tipped his hat. "Good day."

"Oh no, you're staying right here while I get Barnaby."

Clarence kept walking until he got to the door and Cari had to pull it shut as he pushed it.

"It's not safe out there."

"I'll take my chances." He puffed up his chest proudly. More like stupidly, from Carissa's perspective. She shook her head, ready to argue, but someone was coming down the road now that made this situation incrementally worse.

"Get down!" she whispered hoarsely.

"I'm leaving!" He lifted his hand, trying to swat hers away. With only a glass door between them and the outdoors of the Otherworld, Clancy might as well have been wearing a giant piece of cardboard around his neck that read: *catch me, I'm right here.*

"If you'll just let go of the door, I'll be on my—"

Carissa put a hand over Clancy's mouth and dragged him behind a booth. He struggled up to the point where Carissa whispered, "It's a sidhe!" Then, he, too, was still as a frightened dormouse.

Her eyes scanned the red fabric of the booth until the sidhe passed by the bakery windows. Then, she let Clancy go.

"Thank goodness Gooseberry doesn't have a storefront open in the Otherworld. You might stand a chance if you hide out a little while here—until we figure out what to do with you."

"You're going to harbor a fugitive?" He spit out the words as if they were impossible to believe.

Cari placed her hands on her hips. "I happen to think you're innocent. And, I'm helping you because you're Barnaby's cousin, but I don't condone your drinking or sneaking or stealing. Now, we're trying to help you, so if Barnaby's giving you an earful, you might try something different and listen for once."

Clarence grunted, but he also nodded. That was progress. Carissa left him and stealthily made her way across the street. She ducked behind a car parked right across from Gooseberry and watched the sidhe.

It was Varick of Vale, peering into her store window. He disappeared in plain sight, which meant he'd decided to enter the human world. Carissa waited. If Maren were there, she'd let him in, and he'd be distracted. If she wasn't, he might've kept his ability to see in both worlds and would spot her entering Barnaby's.

But so what? She wasn't wanted for anything, and neither was Barnaby. Visiting the leprechaun's shop wasn't a crime. What exactly would she be doing wrong? The only thing that was remotely untoward, from an outsider's perspective, was her hiding like this.

Feeling a little silly, she squared her shoulders and continued to Barnaby's. The door chimed a playful tune as she entered. The bell's announcement of a visitor didn't seem to lift the leprechaun's spirits.

Poor Barnaby sat at the cashier's desk, leaning on the counter with his hand on his cheek. The dejected tailor was a sad sight. He hadn't even seemed to notice Varick across the street. It wasn't like Barn not to snoop with his eyes glued to the window. He didn't even look up when Carissa entered.

She cleared her throat and smiled, determined to lift his spirits. "I have good news."

Barnaby lifted his brooding gaze and pushed himself up from the counter.

"Cari?" The leprechaun scrambled out of his seat and walked around the corner. "What have you found?"

"Clarence. He's in Gooseberry, but Varick is across the street in the human world."

Barnaby walked to the window and peered out. "Varick? No, no, this is bad." He knotted his hands.

Carissa knelt beside him, closing her finger around his. "Don't worry, Barn. I'll go across the street and distract him. You get Clancy and take him somewhere safe."

"But where? He can't come in here; the police have been in here three times already, and Varick is likely to come here."

"Barn, it's okay." She bit her lip. He did have a good point. "I'll go across the street. Give me a minute inside the apothecary and then go to Gooseberry and wait. I'll send Maren, and you tell her to take Clancy to my house."

Nan was off today, so she'd be home. She wouldn't like this surprise, but what else could Cari do?

Carissa started to stand but Barnaby clutched her fingers with both hands.

"Thank you." His eyebrows shot up and conveyed hope and gratitude but, beneath the surface, Cari knew he was wrapped in a knot of anxiety.

He released her hands, and she made her way across the street and into the Seelie Tree Apothecary. Inside, Varick was standing with his arms crossed, intimidating a wide-eyed Maren on the opposite side of the back counter.

"And when do you expect her to be in?" Only Varick could make a question seem like a charge against a guilty person.

"I'm in now," Cari answered.

Varick turned around without uncrossing his arms. The head of a sidhe squadron looked different since she'd last seen him. His blond hair had taken on some brown streaks around his temples. If he were a human, she expected that might translate to grey, although he had to be too young for that. He was, what, two hundred? For a nearly immortal being, or one whose lifespan was far beyond even an elf's, that was nothing. Though his shoulders may have broadened from sword training, he seemed to have otherwise thinned.

His face was too smooth to say he looked like he'd aged. It might've been his expression, but Cari could picture worry lines by his eyes where they would be on a human. She ignored the glaring green eyes and continued up to the counter. Once she was safely around the other side with Varick facing away from the window, she began her charade.

"Oh, darn," Cari set the cornbread down, "I forgot to order a coffee. Maren, would you mind going next door and getting one for me?" She shuffled around in her purse, taking out some money. "Here, you can get something for yourself, too."

Maren's smirk implied that she understood this was a ploy of some kind, but she went along with it. "Sure, no problem."

Then, just to be Maren, she spun on her heels and smiled sweetly at Varick. "Any coffee for you?"

Cari could've sworn a vein pulsed by Varick's temple. Once the gold specks in his green irises became visible, it was time to do something.

Carissa gave Maren a push, not hard enough to hurt her, but hopefully strong enough to send a message. *Humans do not address the sidhe. Ever.*

Maren, with an expression that was still perfectly poised, walked around the counter and out the door. For no other reason than to ruin Carissa's plans, fate happened to bring Cameron Larke to the door just as Maren was leaving.

Carissa could see Barnaby in the background, just leaving for Gooseberry, too. Why he thought this was ideal timing was beyond Cari.

The moment he saw Cameron, Varick dropped his arms, looked up at the ceiling with eyes closed, and muttered, "More humans." That stance meant that he missed the leprechaun tiptoeing across the street.

"Oh, I'm sorry," Cam stopped. He turned sideways as if considering leaving. "Am I interrupting something?"

Varick turned back to Carissa with a set jaw and grabbed the counter like it was all he could do from losing his temper. From the meager length of the counter space, Carissa could see that his eyes were more of a gold hue than usual. She'd seen Varick annoyed plenty of times, this was beyond that. He almost looked ill.

She was about to ask what was wrong, but then she remembered that he was a sidhe and would not welcome the question. Instead, she waited for him to say why he was here.

"I have received a report of a red fae in Fairfield Castle. I'm here to investigate."

Darn that Rolin! It was good to know that the head of the elves wasn't one to keep anything from the sidhe. This wasn't the plan at all.

"Actually, that's why I'm here." Cameron braved the walk to the counter but stayed as far to the other end as he could. "I talked to the mayor about the redcap. He's going to send Father Quinn with some guards there tonight to do a cleansing."

Carissa felt the elf-light swirling around her heart. If she could've shot it out her eyes at Cam, she might've at that moment.

"What?" she exclaimed.

Varick didn't seem to mind the news. "Very well. My guards and I will be on the grounds at dusk."

"Sounds good." Cam's awkward smile beamed false self-assurance. He leaned forward and studied Varick's face. "Hey, are you all right? You don't look well."

Varick's glare silenced him. The sidhe's pounding footsteps resounded all the way to the door.

"Intense as always." Cam patted his forehead with the back of his hand. He stopped when he noticed Carissa's stare. "What?"

"I thought we agreed you wouldn't say anything to the mayor until we spoke to Jane."

"Um…you never specifically said that."

"I shouldn't have to!"

"What was I supposed to do, Cari? The mayor wanted an update, and unless I told him there was another fae there, he was going to go after Clancy. I had to tell him, and then I had to tell him how to solve it."

Carissa looked down, slapping a hand over her eyes.

Cam stepped closer. "We have until tonight. That's more than enough time to get Jane to help Alden. I'll set everything up and meet you at the Everly's this afternoon."

"No," Cari said. She stomped over to the door and locked it. Then she flipped the open sign to closed and marched back to get her things. "We're going there now."

Chapter 15
Tricks, Treats, and Tales

Jane held a bouquet of blue and yellow flowers in front of a headstone in the Everly's private cemetery. Fudge took Carissa and Cameron through the home, past the gardens, and to the graves overlooking the cliff that faced the shore. There, they saw Jane with the flowers, already waiting for them at Alden's grave.

The wind caressed the hem of Jane's skirt. Carissa and Cameron walked up near her but kept a respectful distance so she could mourn privately. Fudge left them alone.

After a while, Jane knelt and placed the flowers in front of the inscription: *Alden Everly, who lives on in other forms.* It was accurate. Whether that was accidental or by intention, Cari wasn't sure. When Jane rose again, Carissa made her way forward. She and Cam stood on either side of Alden's sister.

"Jane?" Carissa asked softly.

"Macara sent us to talk to you," Cam said. "It's, um…it's about your brother. Maybe you want to sit for this."

Jane made no movement.

Cam continued, "Your brother is, was, is, well he's—"

"He's the ankou," Jane finished. Her eyes were fixed on the headstone.

"Cam," Cari whispered. Cameron looked at her, but Carissa's eyes had followed Jane's, who was not looking at the engraving but at a bag sitting beside the stone.

Carissa picked it up and opened it. It was filled with similar ingredients to the summoning spell and more. Cam grabbed the edge of the bag and looked at it too.

"I don't understand," he said. "Did Alden visit you? Or did Macara tell you to do this?"

Jane let out something between a sigh and a sob and put a hand to her face, then she walked back to the garden. Carissa and Cam walked with her to where a cold, grey bench was sitting underneath what looked like a mistletoe tree.

Carissa put an arm around Jane's shoulder until the young woman had composed herself enough to speak.

"I'm learning new things every day. Whether I want to or not. I learned from Miss Morgan before Alden died that he and I are descendants not just of the MacAirts, but the fae, several fae, beginning with a sidhe woman Miss Morgan was particularly attached to named Baírinn. I learned from Varick of Vale when he first saw me at Hela's that the sidhe magic was passed on to me. I learned from Macara after Miss Morgan's death that I am meant to be a druidess. And I learned from her today that my brother is the ankou." She looked at Carissa, teary-eyed. "But I don't want to be a druid. I don't want Alden to be the ankou. I just want all of this to go away."

Jane reached for Carissa, who hugged her while she cried. She shared a pitying look with Cam. Cari didn't know what to say. She could feel for Jane. Magic could be a burden as much as a blessing, especially if one hadn't been carefully trained since birth in its use. But they needed Jane's help.

"Jane," Carissa said when the hug broke. "I know you don't want this all to be true, but it is. Your brother is the ankou, and he needs your help."

Jane clutched something at her chest, a necklace she was wearing. With Jane's fingers wrapped around it, Carissa couldn't see what it was exactly. But when her hand fell away, it revealed the same locket Carissa had seen before, once in Miss Morgan's hands, once on the ground in Vale, and once on the table sitting between Jane and Macara. It was the emblem of a tree.

Carissa wasn't sure what it meant, but if it was tied to her powers the way Cari's own locket was, then it represented this destiny Jane was fighting. No wonder it had been tossed aside in Vale and its presence had upset Jane before. She had thrown it down herself.

Letting go of the locket, Jane stood. She, Cam, and Carissa made their way back to the grave. Cam retrieved the bag once again, and Jane began taking out the materials. She handed Cari the powder for the summoning spell and removed a stick fo herself. In this context, Carissa realized it was a druid wand, but it reminded Cari of the stick Miss Morgan had used for walking. Jane tied mistletoe to the end of it and a string of other assorted herbs to her wrist. Then she instructed Cari to scatter the powder over the grave. Jane began an incantation.

The wind picked up, tossing Jane's dress and hair wildly about. The grey clouds sent down a light drizzle that quickly turned into rain.

"Great," Cam said, holding the now-empty bag over his head for some shelter.

Cari was only barely listening. She could understand some of the old Gaelic Jane was speaking. Jane's hand tingled with magic, bright white magic crackling with silver sparks. That was sidhe magic indeed. Jane looked at Cari, who understood. She put her hands over the grave like Jane was doing, palms facing downward. Her own electric elf-magic streamed from her hands.

"Whoa," Cam uttered. His mouth hung open. His hands held a bag stretched open between them, shielding him at least partly from the water. Rain drenched his overcoat, and the fiery light of fae magic lit his brown eyes in wonder.

Water droplets fell harder on the ground, lightning flashed over the mountain, and the sound of distant thunder rumbled in their ears. Jane and Cari had to shout the final part of the spell.

"Show thee ankou!"

Thunder broke closer than Cari had ever heard it in her life. Lightning flashed almost in unison. The bright light of it turned all three eyes in the direction of where it had struck.

There was the ankou in skeletal form.

Cam's reflexes made him jump back, and he thrust the bag out like a shield. Alden stood, looking straight through them as if he didn't see them at all. His signature black shirt and pants with the hooded jacket made him an even darker figure against the black night. At least his skeletal appearance was fading, and he was returning to the Alden they all knew.

Then he sank to the ground.

As soon as Cam got over the shock, he ran to him. Carissa and Jane followed.

"He's unconscious!" Cam shouted over the din of rain.

Cameron tried to wake him. His hand passed right through his friend's shoulder. Cam's eyes widened, and he looked at his hands and then at Alden.

"I can't help him." There was a mixture of awe and frustration in his shaking voice.

Jane knelt over her brother. Her hand blazed as if in silvery fire. She touched her brother's shoulder just as Cam had done. Hers rested on solid form.

Cam's eyes widened.

"He was like a ghost."

"He's weak from the crossing," Jane said. "Help him into the house."

Cam hoisted Alden up, clumsily, but after a few pulls, he managed to carry much of the ankou's weight on his shoulder and back.

By the time they reached the back door to Jane's living room, the two of them were drenched. Jane didn't seem nearly as wet. Carissa felt almost as awed by her as she had been by

Macara. Cari had wondered the whole time why Macara wasn't here. *Is it because she knew Jane could handle this all herself?*

The thought was barely whispered in her subconscious when Carissa saw Macara sitting indoors in an armchair. Warm as can be and sipping a drink from a teacup, Macara watched Cameron drop Alden onto the plush sofa in front of her. Jane lifted Alden's feet, which Cam had failed to adequately set onto the couch.

Interestingly, beside Macara sat Magnus MacLir, on a chair that had been brought in from the dining room. The Everlys were nowhere in sight. Magnus set down his cup and saucer and motioned for them to sit.

Cam and Cari took the smaller sofa to the side, and Jane took the remaining sofa space beside her brother.

"I'd say they've done an excellent job," Macara said to MacLir.

"They do show promise," MacLir remarked. His eyes ran over the three of them before returning to Macara. "I see what you mean. But the real test might be too much."

"Um," Cam held up a finger as if raising his hand to ask a question, "what 'real' test?"

MacLir leaned toward Macara. "Not very bright," he whispered loud enough for all to hear, which, in Cari's mind, defeated the purpose.

"Brighter than you think," Macara replied.

"Are you talking about me?" Cam asked. He turned toward Carissa. "I think they're talking about me."

Cari put a hand on Cam's to calm him. "What next?" she asked, but Jane interrupted.

"He's waking."

Alden groaned, putting a hand to his head. Stirring from the couch like that, slowly sitting up, Cari could have easily fooled herself into thinking that he was somehow alive again. She sat at the edge of her seat. Cam gripped the arm of the sofa.

"Alden." He grinned like a kid seeing his friend for the first time after coming home from summer camp.

Alden came to, gaining awareness of his surroundings. He looked at each face in the room until his eyes rested on his sister.

"Jane." He seemed surprised, even more so when she hugged him. His eyes widened and slowly his arms closed around her.

"I've missed you," he said.

She was too choked up to reply. They broke the hug. Alden brought his hands away, looking at them.

"I feel the warmth." He looked at the roaring fire. "I can smell the cinnamon apple." His eyes rested on Macara's tea. He looked up at her and MacLir. "How is that possible?"

"Jane cast a spell, I believe," Macara explained.

"He was weak. The grounding wasn't enough," Jane said.

"Well done," Macara praised. Her eyes found Alden's. "She's given you a greater connection to the human world than you had with only the power of an ankou. When her spell fades, the feeling of being alive will fade with it." Macara returned to sipping her tea.

"It should last only an hour or so," MacLir waved off the miracle with a flick of his fingers. "It will take that much time for your powers to readjust from your return. You really ought to drink that." He pointed to a gold cup Cari hadn't previously noticed on the coffee table. "It'll restore your ankou powers, which on their own are more powerful at this time of year than any other." MacLir waggled his eyebrows. "All Hallows' Eve."

Jane dabbed her eyes with a handkerchief, disinterested in anything but her brother's return. Cari's mind was spinning a web of ideas, connecting everything from the last few days.

"You were in the world beyond like the person in the story. Drinking from the cup brings you back."

"Not back to life," Macara emphasized, "back to this realm."

"All right, so it brings you back. And you," she looked at MacLir, "you sent him there to, what, teach him something?"

"I don't know," MacLir said innocently. "Did you learn anything?" he asked Alden.

"Wait," Cam said, "I'm not following." He pointed at MacLir. "*You* sent him to the realm of the dead?"

"He's the stranger in the story Jane told about the MacAirts." Carissa gathered she was right from the fact that no one other than Cam looked shocked in any way. Macara had practically given it away at dinner. He liked to hear the stories of the old days, in this case meaning the days of their ancestors, because he was in them.

"You're the real MacLir? The Manann MacLir from the fae archives?" Cam put it together.

Magnus smiled. "Definite promise," he said to Macara.

"I did tell you." Macara seemed pleased.

But Cari felt anger sparking her elf-light. "Why the games? You're playing with us like we're nothing."

"No," Macara took a defensive tone.

"Not at all." MacLir picked up his cup and hovered a hand over it, light radiating from it like a dark blue mist. It almost looked like ink in water. Carissa couldn't place that kind of magic. What was MacLir?

Cam shuddered. Carissa was more curious than afraid. Her eyes were drawn to the cup. She could see the steam rising from it.

"Enough of this," Alden said. "I did what you asked of me. Whatever you're doing in Moss Hill, you don't have to be here anymore."

MacLir's eyebrows nearly touched together. "Of course I do, I have a business transaction with Mr. O'Brien. I plan to see it through."

Carissa parted her lips, but she wasn't sure what to make of that. Whatever MacLir's business with O'Brien was, it centered on the castle. But O'Brien hadn't seemed very willing to work with the town's or MacLir's, plans for it. So, was MacLir still hoping O'Brien would recover? Or was he hoping he wouldn't?

"What did he ask you to do?" Jane asked Alden.

Alden looked at MacLir, but the man was giving no sign as to whether the ankou should answer. Reluctantly, Alden told

Jane, "The previous ankou didn't want to leave Moss Hill. I had to force him back to the world beyond."

"And are you certain you succeeded?" MacLir asked.

"Yes," Alden replied.

"Good," MacLir said. "So the previous ankou is in the world beyond. I'd say it's about time to make sure a certain red fae is banished there too, wouldn't you say?"

"Wait," Cam said. "There really was a redcap and an ankou on the castle grounds the night O'Brien was pushed?" His eyes moved briefly to Cari. "Or fell," he had to add.

Carissa was too preoccupied to argue.

"Which one might have pushed O'Brien?" she asked.

"The redcap, the ankou, both of them. Does it matter?" MacLir asked.

"Yes," Cari replied.

"Why?" MacLir challenged.

Carissa's jaw fell.

Jane responded. "You have to banish the red fae no matter what. It's dangerous."

Cari looked at the large clock sitting on the wall above the fireplace as Jane explained to Alden about the priest. Fifteen minutes to six meant the priest would be starting soon with his banishment of the redcap.

Cam, Jane, and Alden stood.

"Uh, shouldn't Alden stay here?" Cam asked.

"As long as the priest doesn't target him specifically, he'll be fine," Jane said.

"We should make sure the priest is safe," Alden said. "Above all, he needs to be protected if he stands a chance of banishing a fae spirit."

Alden's eyes moved to Carissa, who was still sitting on the sofa. Everyone turned to her. She could see them in her periphery, but her attention was on the cup. She wasn't just thinking of the priest's well-being. She'd made a promise to Mrs. O'Brien to keep her husband safe. MacLir had told her that between herself, Jane, and the MacAirts, she had everything she needed to do that. She understood now what she had to do. Before she stood, Carissa made a request of Jane.

"There are a few things I need to borrow before we go."

MacLir showed his approval with a smirk. When he spoke, Cari wasn't sure if he was addressing her or Macara.

"Not nothing at all, but the future of Moss Hill stands here in my sight."

Macara answered, "In faith, I do believe you're right."

Chapter 16
Spirits and Spells

Father Quinn held his black hat against his head as he fought the wind in front of the castle. He lingered beneath the gates a moment, shaking the water off his coat on top of his robes.

Carissa was the first to spot him from the uppermost window of the west side of the castle where Alden had brought her, Cameron, and Jane. The room itself had been some kind of watch station, bare except for a few scattered plates of armor leftover from times long forgotten.

This being Jane's first trip with Alden's powers of teleportation, she was a little woozy, especially since they stopped at the hospital first. While Alden attended to her, Carissa opened the window, causing a cloud of dust to take to the air.

Cameron sneezed. "Ugh, Cari, what are you doing?"

"The air in here has to be a hundred years old." Carissa coughed. "We need fresh air for Jane."

"Yeah, but it's raining," he argued. "It's not air you're letting in. It's water."

"Shh!" She leaned forward. She could hear the mayor bellowing below.

"What are you waiting for?"

"It's prudent to wait for it to stop raining!"

Carissa could see Belkin in the center of the courtyard, at least she assumed it was him under the grey umbrella.

"The sidhe will be here any minute, Father. You'll want to get started before they take over. You don't want them trying to protect the redcap, do you?"

Carissa couldn't believe what she was hearing. She put a hand on her hip. "Why would the mayor say that? No sidhe would protect a dark fae."

"What are you talking about? And why does it sound like you're accusing him of something?"

Cam hadn't heard over the rain. It was only Cari's elf ears that made that possible, she realized.

She saw Father Quinn entering the courtyard. He was clearly uncomfortable, ducking and running while an officer held an umbrella over his head. Belkin could have at least offered him an umbrella of his own. Two more officers followed. Eventually, the group disappeared inside the main castle building.

From this part of the castle, she had a clear view of the section of the rampart wall from which O'Brien had fallen. Carissa took advantage of that to see what she could of the walkway. She peered as far over the rampart walls as possible. It was useless in the heavy rain.

"You're blocking the window," Cameron pointed out.

She stepped back. "Can't see anything anyway. Alden, we need to get to a better spot."

Jane, who was better now, held a hand up and looked to her side. "We're not alone," she whispered.

"I don't like the sound of that." Cam looked around the old room with a wary eye. Dust and spiderwebs covered every corner.

Cam shuddered. Carissa patted his arm to show she understood. He was handling it extremely well. If she had a fear of spiders like Cam did, she probably would want out of this room as soon as possible too. There was not, however, any sign of a person, fae or otherwise, besides the four of them.

"I'll lead us down," Alden volunteered.

"Not a moment too soon." Cam leapt over an artifact, a shield of some sort.

Alden and Jane walked to the doorway and began down the steps first. Cam didn't hesitate to keep in line right after them.

Carissa, however, took one last glance out the window. The rain was letting up. Outside, she could see the priest and the others at the top of the rampart. They were close enough that she could see his purple stole and the vial of holy water in his hands.

"Lord, have mercy…" she heard him begin.

She almost didn't want to leave. From up here, she could see the priest clearly enough that if something were to try to attack the group, she might be able to extend her elf-light just enough to help. It was better for her and Cam to walk right up and help them, even if that meant separating from Alden, who shouldn't be seen. But what if they didn't reach the top of the wall in time? What if the redcap attacked before she had a chance to make it there?

She breathed a sigh of relief when she saw Varick and the sidhe entering through the gatehouse. They could see the priest from there and the powers of a sidhe had farther reach than all but the most experienced of elves. She could walk down now without fear.

Almost the second she thought that, she heard something. That sensation of something moving in her periphery occurred as it had before. She should've left with the others. She turned her head. No one was there. Jane had said they weren't alone. She steadied her hands on the window frame, gathering courage.

She turned, ready to strike. Her hands sparkled in front of her with the glow of her elf-light. Still, no one was in sight. She dropped her hands and took a moment to calm herself. She was still on guard, but she neither saw nor heard anything in the room.

Until she felt it push her.

What "it" was she couldn't see clearly, but it was definitely two hands she felt grab her arms and fling her out the window. She felt like a rag doll in the air. She didn't see it but knew her head missed the top of the window by centimeters. Helplessly, she watched her feet following as she flung her arms up in a hopeless attempt to catch the frame. Her scream must've caught every eye in the area. But what could anyone do?

Nothing, if there had only been humans around. Lucky for her, there was an ankou to catch her and disappear into thin air. They reappeared back at the base of the castle by the stairway where Cam and Jane were standing.

"Are you okay?" Cam gripped her arms and searched her face. The moment she nodded, he pulled her too tightly into a hug.

"I'm fine!" she croaked as she gasped for breath.

He let go only enough to say to her, "You scared me to death!" before pulling her back into a hug.

"Okay, you can let me go now," she said. When she finally managed to assure him that she was fine, she realized that things were about to be very much the opposite for the friend who'd just saved her.

"They've seen you," Carissa said to Alden. They, all three, knew what that meant for him if the priest decided to specifically direct his attention to him. But Alden wasn't focused on them, he was standing at the entryway to the castle, his eyes searching the whole courtyard and walls above.

He was searching for Jane. Carissa realized she was not with them. Cameron realized it, too.

"She was just here." Cam scratched his head. His eyes widened again, looking at Alden. "You don't think the red fae's got her?"

"Protect the priest!" Varick's order carried over the wind. The footfalls of the sidhe guards echoed in the courtyard.

Varick himself appeared at the door. Alden stepped back. Cameron, to his credit, stepped between them. "Alden's not the one haunting this castle, Varick, uh, sir. The red fae—"

"Stay here," Varick commanded. He neither seemed to hear nor care about what Cam had said. He also didn't seem to care about the ankou. Instead, he looked at Carissa. "Come with me."

Carissa gave a look to Cameron to show that she would be okay. Varick wouldn't wait even that long for her. Cari had to jog three steps to catch up.

"How can I help?" she asked as they speed-walked up the stairs.

"Get your friend out of harm's way."

Carissa assumed he meant Jane, which meant she was currently in harm's way. The top of the rampart walls was a fire fight—quite literally. The moment they reached the top of the stairs, Carissa could see a circle of sidhe guards surrounding the priest. Though she'd been glad that the rain had let up, right now they probably could've used it.

The sidhe were using their magic as shields, deflecting fire being thrown at them by an angry fae spirit. Carissa couldn't see it clearly. Only flashes of red and orange caught her eye.

In an effort to trace the redcap, her eyes turned to Jane, who was standing in front of the mayor. She might've been protecting him. He was peering over her shoulder with a look of sheer horror on his face.

Jane's eyes were closed, but her hands in front of her were swirling a growing sphere of blue light between them. If it was like her elf-light, then Cari knew exactly what Jane was doing. If they could keep the redcap from attacking Jane, then the light she was building could be used to strike down the fae spirit at precisely the right moment in the priest's prayer. Carissa wasn't sure exactly what moment that was, but she was willing to help in warding off the redcap for as long as she could.

She took a hurried step forward only to be pulled back by Varick's arm. He seemed to know exactly what she was thinking.

"Any of us can do what she is doing. She's not needed here. Get her out." He let go and rushed to the center of the circle, blasting at the redcap with green energy from his hands as he went. He was right beside the priest in a moment.

Carissa had her orders. The question now was whether she obeyed his command or that of her own gut. There was no choice. Jane was new at being a druidess. The sidhe, on the other hand, were too powerful to fight against. She hoped that was as true for the redcap as it was for her.

She ran toward Jane, ducking to avoid a blast of fiery wrath. Red light did reach toward Jane, but it couldn't cut through whatever shield she was creating with her hands.

"Jane!" Carissa shouted.

Jane kept her eyes closed. She either hadn't heard her or was too deep in concentration to acknowledge Cari's shouting.

"Cari!" Carissa heard a voice ring out behind her. She swirled around to see Cameron, holding a dusty shield and running like he had no clue how to use it. He kept flinching like he was about to be hit by some invisible force.

"Cam, what are you doing here?" Carissa could have killed him for being so reckless.

"Protecting you," he said once they were face to face.

It was a sweet sentiment, but the stupidest thing she'd heard from him in her life. Now she understood how Varick felt, with someone he cared for rushing into danger like that.

Her heart was already beating fiercely in her chest. She couldn't consciously process that thought. She did, however, with some surprise, take note of the feeling she had in that instant. It was a split second of fear upon realizing that she didn't know what she would do if something happened to Cam.

She gasped, pulling him back as fire hit his shield. Both of them braced themselves with one foot stepping back to cushion the blow. Pain shot through her wrist. She grabbed her hand, her face contorting in pain.

"Are you okay?" Cam dropped his shield to ask. Carissa pulled it back up with her good hand.

"Keep your guard up." She knew there was no point in telling him to go back. He had a reckless streak in him that meant the worst decision making at times like these.

Carissa turned her attention back to Jane. The blue energy around her had expanded outward and flattened to become a shield in itself. It swirled around her and the mayor to deflect anything that came her way. Nothing seemed to be directed at her. Rather, Varick was actively deflecting any attack in her direction. Unlike the other sidhe, who defended the priest with their energies, Varick was attacking the redcap with his green light in blasts that nearly caught him each time. Carissa had the impression that, instead of Varick keeping the redcap occupied, it was the fae who was keeping Varick distracted while he continued to assault the group from every direction.

From the scowl on Varick's face and the gold of his eyes, Cari determined it was best to get Jane out as soon as possible. She and Cam used the shield to make their way to Jane's side.

"Jane, we have to get out of here."

She kept her eyes closed. "Not yet. Almost ready." She didn't seem to be speaking loudly, but Carissa heard her clearly over the ruckus.

"No, you're in danger."

Carissa's words were like a prophecy. The next second, the redcap appeared by Jane's side. Varick's magic hit the fae squarely in the chest. He screeched so loudly Cameron dropped the shield to cover his ears. Carissa covered hers and cringed.

The redcap rolled to his knees right in front of him. Cari recoiled as he lifted his head. He was a surprisingly small figure. He did wear a red cap, and he had thick, broad shoulders. Carissa could see how upon first glance he might be mistaken for Clancy.

But only if Clancy were a horrifying evil version of himself. His sharp, overset teeth, talon-like hands, tangled, matted hair—even the unnatural tint of his crimson hat—were all ghastly. He set his eyes on Carissa and she could feel Cam's hand wrap around her arm to pull her back. Her heart beat enough elf-light directly to her fingers that the mere reflex of crossing her arms out in front of her resulted in a blast of electric light.

Suddenly, she, Cam, and Jane were transported to a place farther along the wall. It was a little, covered area of the rampart, one away from the battle and from sight. Alden stood with them.

Cam let go of Cari and uttered, "Oh, I think I'm going to be sick."

Carissa closed her eyes thankfully. When she opened them again, Jane was still standing as before. Carissa reached out, trying to tell her that she was safe. She didn't need to create more light. Mid-reach, she was glad Jane hadn't stopped.

In front of them, the redcap appeared, talons drawn. Though he was a half-man in stature, his presence was wholly disarming.

A flash of light caused the apparition to blink and all of their heads to turn. Farther down the walkway was Reginald, camera in hand.

"I knew it!" he exclaimed. He had to have come up the wall from the other side of the castle. "I knew this town was Hy Brasil, and now I have proof." He walked closer until he was almost in the covered area with them. "I knew it wasn't lightning I was seeing."

"Stay back!" Cam held his hand out for Reg to stop.

The tourist kept walking. "I got lost three times in the Vale woods and have been camping here every night, but it was worth it!" He held up the camera, unaware of just how much danger he was in.

The redcap snarled. Only then did Reg's eyes widen and his mouth quiver. The red fae leapt. Reg made to turn only to slip and fall, knocking himself out on the pavement. Alden disappeared and re-constituted himself between Reg and the red fae. The redcap hit Alden's forearm and he was thrust back, landing on the ground in front of Cam with a loud enough thud that he must not have had time to desolidify.

Cam pulled Carissa back behind him. She moved forward. She wasn't about to let him shield her when she was the one better able to defend them.

"He's breathing, but just barely," Alden shouted.

Carissa was glad he was all right, but her attention wasn't on the fallen tourist. The priest's voice grew louder as the sounds of fighting ceased on their end of the wall. The sidhe were no longer in battle with the fae because he was here, with them. Only, as terrifying as he was, he also looked weakened by the priest's prayer. He had his eyes fixed on Cameron.

Don't be afraid, Carissa realized.

Outside, he'd been after the mayor. As soon as Reginald saw him, his fear had clearly been more intense than anyone else in the group. Now, he was after Cam. The redcap was going after the person in the group who was most frightened. "Don't be afraid," she told them. "He wants you to be afraid. He feeds on it."

The redcap looked at her, angered by her advice. Then it screeched in agony. The priest's words could be heard loud and clear. Jane's eyes flung open. Like the sidhe, they were gold when using magic.

She spun the blue light in her hands. It was large enough now to envelop the fae. The next moment, it began to shrink. The gold in Jane's eyes flickered. "Something's draining my power," Jane's voice wavered.

Carissa stepped forward, putting her arms out. Alden shifted to skeletal form and blocked the redcap's attempt to launch. The red fae snarled and turned back. He froze, immobilized. Screeching his protest, the fae was helpless to do anything else. With Cari and Jane's magic combined, the blue and green light surrounded the redcap. He could not move to escape the priest's prayer.

"...Forever and ever. Amen."

Cari held her hands in front of her eyes as a blaze of white light enveloped the blue and green. The redcap was gone.

They stood in shock. A smile started to spread across Cam's face.

He swept Jane up in a hug. "You did it!" he said, twirling her in the air. She returned the hug with the rare sound of laughter. Alden's lips drew upward. He nodded at his sister. A small gesture, but it showed how proud he was of her. Carissa laughed as Cameron turned to her with a grin.

"Is it over?" a voice yelled across the ramparts. It was the mayor. A sliver of fear still snaked through his voice.

Carissa looked at the group. They looked over at Reginald, but there was no one on the ground. Cameron broke from the group to get a closer look.

"He's gone," Cam said.

Cari bit her lip. Having seen what he did and caught it on camera, there was no telling what Reginald would do. But that was a worry for another day. Carissa, Cam, and Jane left the confined area to make their way back to the others. Varick looked relieved upon seeing them.

"Cameron." The mayor looked between the three of them. "And you both. I suppose I should thank you for protecting me from the fae."

Carissa looked at Jane. Her face was red and she didn't seem to be eager to say anything.

"We're glad you're all right," Carissa jumped in.

"The redcap is gone," Cam added.

"But there wasn't just the redcap," the mayor said. He turned to the priest. "Did you also banish the ankou?"

The priest replied in puzzlement, "I wasn't aware of an ankou."

Carissa thanked her lucky stars. He might've been too deep in the prayer to have seen him.

"He was here," the mayor insisted. "I know it. I saw two of them. The redcap was up here, but you," he pointed at Cari, "you fell out the window and the ankou snatched you up."

Cari froze. This was bad. She had to think of something.

"Sir, I did fall, but...." She floundered, looking for an explanation.

Varick stepped in, "It was my magic that saved her." He looked at Carissa. Lying was difficult for an elf but, apparently, not so for a sidhe.

"No, I saw a form," the mayor said, but he didn't sound so certain anymore. With Varick's green and gold tinted eyes locked on him, he couldn't continue arguing. "I guess if you say so...I, I must've been mistaken."

"Cari, Cameron, Jane, come here," Father Quinn said. They all gathered closer. The priest splashed holy water on each of their faces. "There," he said. "Now that's done. I think we can call it a day." He winked at Cari.

Her lips parted. Had Father Quinn known Alden was there all along? And had she just seen the head of the sidhe guard protecting the ankou? What a strange night this had turned out to be. At least it had turned out all right.

They left the castle grounds. Cari was fairly pleased with everything. That is, until she happened to glance up and see Alden standing atop the gatehouse. The look on his face told her somehow this wasn't over.

Chapter 17
Web of Lies

L ater that night, after returning from the battle at Fairfield, Carissa imagined the kitchen would still be quite a mess. Barnaby, Nan, Clancy, and Maren had been busy baking their fall-themed treats while the rest of the group was out.

Cari went to bed, exhausted, not looking forward to the cleanup in the morning.

***

When she came downstairs for breakfast the next day, the place was spotless.

"Good morning, Cari!" Barnaby lifted his coffee by way of greeting.

"Morning, Barn. What are you doing here?" Carissa poured some of the freshly brewed coffee into her mug. She usually drank tea in the mornings, but there were some days she needed something stronger. If ever there was a day like that, it was today.

"Clancy and I stayed over on the couch and guest room. I hope that's all right," Barnaby answered.

"Sure, though I hope the sofa was comfortable."

"I wouldn't know. I took the guest room."

Cari chortled along with Barnaby.

"What's all this laughing about?" Nan exited her bedroom directly into the kitchen.

"Only that Clancy is still asleep on the couch."

"You can laugh." Nan took the last of the coffee. "You didn't have to hear his snoring all night."

"I don't snore." Clancy wandered in, scratching his backside and yawning.

Cari kept her laughter to herself this time. "I've got to be going. There's something important I have to do before work this morning." She heaved the fancy purple velvet bag from the Everly's onto her shoulder.

"Ahem." Barnaby pushed Clancy forward as he approached the table.

"What?" He took a defensive pose. Barnaby lifted his chin and directed his eyes to Cari, clearing his throat again. "Oh, right."

The clurichaun walked up to Carissa and took a small bow. "Thank you for helping me." For the first time ever, she saw Clancy smile. "I really do appreciate you letting me stay in your home last night."

She matched his grin. "You're very welcome, Clancy. And you don't have to worry about anything. I'd say the mayor will officially be announcing your innocence soon."

His eyes widened. "Yippee!" He jumped and then hugged her, squeezing so hard she barely could breathe. "This is magnificent!" He let her go. "A second chance and you'll see," he looked at everyone in the room, "I'll be a new clurichaun now."

Carissa felt rather pleased with herself as she said goodbye and made her way out the door. Taking her usual mode of transportation, she bicycled through the streets and to the apothecary shop. There, she mixed a tonic for the most challenging case she would ever have to treat. It was time to make good on her promise to Mrs. O'Brien.

***

Mr. O'Brien lay in his hospital bed, looking even thinner than before. Carissa took the branch and gold goblet she had borrowed from Jane's out of the bag she'd brought from the Everly's. The goblet and the branch from MacLir's story were not just symbols of the MacAirt family history, they were real.

Now, in her hands, she shook the branch over the comatose patient. A cloud of glittering magic rained down onto him. Nothing happened, but then, it was supposed to make a patient sleep and heal. Maybe it needed time? She used her elf-light to sense the magic working. Gasping, she pulled her hand away.

There was magic already on him. What kind? Even as she pondered it, the branch began its work. He breathed deeper. Color returned to his face. Still, he did not awaken.

She placed the herbal tonic she'd mixed at the Seelie Tree Apothecary and poured it into the chalice. She'd planned to use it to wake him after healing him with the branch. She wasn't sure if she still should. But he did look better than before. The tonic glowed bright orange and sparkled as the spices mixed with the magical effect of the cup. Whatever magic was on him, it seemed to be an old spell. It did not seem to affect the working of the branch.

Gently, she lifted O'Brien's head and poured the liquid down his throat. He reflexively drank until there was no more in the goblet. She set his head down on the pillow again.

Lifting a napkin to clean out the inside of the cup, she was surprised to see that the cup was dry. She put the branch into the bag MacLir had given her.

Her timing could not have been more perfect. Voices outside indicated that Mrs. O'Brien had arrived. Cari stood as the doorknob turned and a figure entered the room.

"Oh," Mrs. O'Brien's lips formed the letter as much as the word. "Carissa, I didn't know you were visiting this morning."

"I've just come to see what I could do." She touched the velvety black bag strung on her shoulder.

Mrs. O'Brien stepped forward. "And?" Her eyes shone with hope.

Carissa restrained her smile. She didn't know yet if her reasoning was correct. MacLir had been so cryptic about whether the branch would heal him and the goblet would wake him. "I gave him a tonic," she said, which was the truth. "That's all I can do."

Mrs. O'Brien nodded. "Thank you for trying."

Carissa walked forward, placing a hand on the woman's shoulder. "I should be getting back to the apothecary shop." She gave a gentle squeeze of reassurance, then made her way to the door.

"Mmm," Mr. O'Brien stirred in his sleep. Then, miraculously, he moved a hand to his forehead. "Mary?" he asked. Mrs. O'Brien rushed over. "Where am I?"

Tears cascading down her cheeks, Mrs. O'Brien laughed and clutched his resting hand in hers. She turned her head toward Cari with grateful eyes. Carissa nodded, then left the two to a joyful reunion.

Her mind wandering all the way down and out of the lobby, thinking about the magic on O'Brien, Carissa passed a memorable tourist with his camera hung at his neck and a tablet in his hand. He was near the point of a tantrum, jabbing at a tablet when Cari walked over. She folded her arms.

"Reginald? What are you doing here?" Then, recalling that he'd been injured the last time she saw him, she asked, "Are you hurt?"

He barely acknowledged her concern, not even looking up as he said, "I fell off my bicycle last night. I guess I must've hit my head." He rubbed his hair, taking a breath. "How about you?"

"I was visiting Mr. O'Brien," Cari said. Then, because she didn't immediately see the harm in saying so, she added, "He's finally woken up this morning."

Reginald didn't seem much interested. He kept flipping through the tablet screens.

"This can't be right. All the articles are gone. The writer has replaced them with this." He gestured toward the device with one hand while waving it wildly with the other.

Carissa kept her eyes on him but reached for the device. He relinquished it to her hands. She read the headline from Tilly's latest blog post: "Halloween Imaginations Run Wild?"

She continued to read the passage to herself. *"Those who know Moss Hill understand that stories of the people of Vale have circulated for centuries, blown to outstanding proportions recently. The idea that spirits walk among us is enticing to believe at this time of year. As much as we, as a culture, have faith in such things, recent events have overexaggerated the existence of apparitions. While it is true that the local priest has blessed the castle, it's also true that this would not have been necessary if not for the townsfolk's panic over what was essentially an accident.*

'Father Quinn blessed the castle today without incident. All went well, and I am confident that the celebrations can continue as originally planned,' said Mayor Belkin."

"I don't believe it for a second," Reginald said. "I'm willing to bet that those who've been there would tell a different story."

"Those who've been there?"

Carissa handed back the tablet. She didn't allow a flicker of emotion to pass over her face. Inside, she was happy that overall, the article seemed to be dismissing the existence of anything remotely supernatural. She was also happy that Reginald didn't seem to remember the events of the night before. But why wouldn't he remember?

She ventured cautiously for an answer, "Were you at the castle last night?"

"No." His free hand clenched into a fist. "If I had been, you can be sure I'd tell the truth, not this rubbish." He stuffed his tablet into a satchel sitting on the chair beside him.

He must've hit his head harder than any of them realized. That was concerning. She should ask a more experienced elf to take a look at healing him before he left the island. The memory might be lost, which worked in their favor, but she didn't want him to be hurt on their account.

She frowned. Reg still had the camera. She caught a glance at the lens before he zipped the bag up.

Nonchalantly, she asked, "Are you all right?" She was sure he would answer that he had a head injury.

Reginald pouted. "Yeah, I'm fine—physically. Not so sure about mentally." He clutched his head. A look of pain flit across his face.

She put a hand on his shoulder. "I'm so sorry to hear that. I hope you feel better soon."

She moved her hand ever-so-slightly down toward where she knew the camera would be and shot a spark from the tip of her finger through to the bottom of the satchel. She could only use her magic on technology for one purpose: to fry it. She'd never seen that as a particularly useful skill—until now.

Reg began a "thank you," and ended it with a relatively troublesome look of realization on his face. For a brief moment, her heart paused between breaths, thinking he'd somehow detected what she'd done. Fortunately, that was not the case.

"Since Mr. O'Brien is awake," Reginald said, "I may as well talk to him. He would know the truth."

Carissa pulled back. She just barely kept her eyebrows from rising. "I don't think he's in any condition to answer any questions, and you're probably not in a condition to ask them."

"I'm fine. Besides, Mrs. O'Brien will agree to speak with me after I tell her who I am."

Carissa raised an eyebrow. "Who is that?" She'd only thought of him as a crazy tourist. It hadn't occurred to her that there might be more to him than that.

Reginald puffed out his chest, "An accomplished attorney of The Smith and CuCullen Law Firm."

Carissa gave him a look of skepticism.

Reginald deflated, "I may have overstated my position. I'm a lawyer." He looked like he was barely twenty-two, far too young to be a lawyer. "Or, I will be soon. Anyway, I'll tell her I'd be willing to take a look at her husband's case."

"I'm fairly sure misrepresenting yourself is a crime."

Reginald took on an indignant tone, "I'm not misrepresenting anything. My father's firm really can take on the case."

"What case?"

"The case of his injury. I'm pretty sure his wife will tell me if someone pushed him—or if she thinks it was something supernatural."

"You really still think there's a mystery here?"

He pushed up his glasses. "I'm sure of it. And I'm not leaving this town until I get to the bottom of it."

He walked off toward the welcome desk to determine the location of Mr. O'Brien's room. Carissa slid next to him while he waited for the receptionist to get off the phone. This time, she tried a friendlier approach.

"All right," she said.

He glanced sideways.

"If there's a mystery, count me in. I just came from Mr. O'Brien's. I'd be happy to show you to his room."

He studied her a moment, apparently uncertain whether to trust her. Finally, he nodded. "Thank you."

The elevator dinged and Cari smiled. Inside she was biting her tongue. Carissa wanted so very much to say anything to get Reg off the trail of any mystery, but he was persistent. She suddenly became hyperaware of the magical items in the bag on her shoulder. Hopefully, he wouldn't ask.

On the right floor, they turned and made their way back to the room. Inside, Mr. O'Brien was sitting up, talking with the doctor and Mrs. O'Brien. The doctor, finished with his checkup, shook O'Brien's hand and walked to the door.

"It's a miracle," he exclaimed upon seeing Cari and Reg.

Carissa bit her lip. Her strained smile failed at that moment.

"Miss Shea, I think I have you to thank for my revival."
Mr. O'Brien's eyes twinkled with gratitude while Mrs. O'Brien
beamed beside him.

Reginald did a half-turn, mouth open, eyes questioning.
Carissa felt her cheeks turning red. Her grip on the rope
tightened. "I didn't do anything," she said.

"Nonsense," Mrs. O'Brien said. "She's the best apothecary
in two hundred years."

Every passing second was another centimeter higher that
Reginald's eyebrows hiked toward his unusually high hairline.
Cari wished they would stop speaking about miracles and
cures. Reginald introduced himself and went right into his
question.

"What would you say attacked you?"

"Attacked me?"

"Yes," Reginald sat in the chair opposite Mrs. O'Brien,
without an invitation to do so. "Well, we have to know whom
to sue, don't we?"

Carissa gritted her teeth. Sue? Not only was he pretending
to be a lawyer, now he was an aggressive one. Reg caught her
eyes and glanced away. She crossed her arms. If he was
nervous, he ought to be.

Mr. O'Brien seemed to notice her movement and turned
his face toward her. She gave him pleading look, silently
beckoning him not to say anything.

"Well," Mr. O'Brien's eyes moved between them, "I don't
know. I don't remember it too clearly."

"Did you see anyone suspicious? Someone strange looking,
with a red hat perhaps, or a skeletal face?"

Mr. O'Brien's face contorted. He paled as if spooked by the
question. "A skeletal face?"

Mrs. O'Brien, seemingly surprised by the line of
questioning, changed subjects. "My husband has just awoken
from a coma. This isn't the best time. Perhaps we could
resume a discussion another day."

"Of course." Reginald snapped to his feet. He had a way
of making the most mundane motions seem awkward. He

pushed his glasses up to the bridge of his nose. "You have my card. If you don't contact me in a few days, I'll contact you."

The O'Briens smiled graciously, but Cari would've taken that as a threat. Reginald reached for Mr. O'Brien's hand and O'Brien obliged. Reg swayed on his feet. Cari set the bag down and put her arms out in case he fell. He brought a hand to his forehead and removed his glasses.

"What's wrong?" Carissa asked.

"N-nothing." Reginald set the frames back on his nose. "Just my head. Still a little sore, I think. I'd better go."

Reginald started toward the door, and Cari turned to leave as well. Mr. O'Brien called her back. She smiled as Reginald passed her.

"Carissa," Mr. O'Brien said when the three of them were alone, "I wasn't really aware of things while I was in my coma." Cari saw the tension on his face as he said the word coma. She could imagine how strange that must sound. "Do people really think it was the ankou that caused me to fall?"

Cari was taken aback by the question. If Mr. O'Brien had pieced that together from the single clue of "*a skeletal face,*" he was sharper than Carissa had known. Or, he'd seen the ankou himself.

"Um, no, sir," she responded. "They thought it was a fae."

She didn't clarify whom. If she told Mr. O'Brien of the redcap, it would only serve to scare him. If he hadn't seen the redcap before, it would be better if he never gave room for such a spirit to haunt him in his dreams.

"Did they catch him?" O'Brien asked.

Cari nodded.

"Good, good." He looked down, seemingly deep in thought.

"Sir, now that Mr. Smith isn't here, you can tell me. Do you know who pushed you?"

Mr. O'Brien closed his eyes and leaned back against his pillow.

"I'm so very tired suddenly," he said. "I must rest."

Remedy and Ruins

Mrs. O'Brien laid her husband's hand down and walked with Carissa to the door.

"I don't know how to thank you." She reached for a hug.

"It was nothing, really." Cari returned the embrace.

Her eyes lingered on the door. A cloud passed over Carissa's face. She didn't know Mr. O'Brien well. There may have been something strange about his whole demeanor, or that might've been part of his normal personality. Or he was just exhausted and she was making too much of it.

She tried returning to her warm expression as she parted from Mrs. O'Brien. The woman's gratitude was genuine enough as they said goodbye. By the time she left the hospital, Carissa's rational mind was convinced she only imagined that something was wrong. It didn't stop the nagging feeling, though.

***

Back in the Seelie Tree Apothecary, Carissa had the pleasure of giving Maren the happy news about the celebrations being back on. Maren didn't seem as happy as she'd expected. Her assistant and friend met her with a stern hand clamped down on the counter.

"Thank you so much for making me an accessory to harboring a criminal."

Carissa tried to respond, but Maren held a finger up to silence her.

"I had to spend an afternoon with a starry-eyed clurichaun making googly eyes at me."

"I'm sorry, I thought you took him and Barnaby to Nan's?"

"She was out, so I had to stay with them a while before she got back."

"He was there this morning. I only saw him for a second, but he seemed happy."

"Oh, he was happy all right. He's my new partner for the baking competition."

"What? How did that happen?"

Maren sighed, dropping her hand away from the counter. "I suggested he carve a pumpkin for the Gooseberry contest, a perfectly good idea that he liked well enough. But Barnaby found out that I was joining the baking contest and insisted that Clancy had a knack for picking the right ingredients for pies. He did make a few good suggestions. Nan said she preferred to stay home and pass out candy as opposed to attending the celebrations, and even Chaos took to Clancy right away. It was like a conspiracy. Long story short, Clancy is joining both the baking and pumpkin carving competitions."

Carissa smiled to herself. Barnaby was trying everything he could to help his cousin be more sociable. This was just one more opportunity for him to make friends and be part of the community. Maren knew it, or she wouldn't have agreed to his helping her in the contest.

"Well, thank you." Carissa wrapped an arm around Maren's shoulder and squeezed. The hug was met with a half-smile half-scowl, and that was the best she was going to get out of Maren. "And you don't have to worry about him being a criminal," Cari added. "The mayor found out another fae was involved and O'Brien's awake now, so I'm sure he'll clear Clancy's name."

"Oh good," sarcasm seeped into Maren's tone, "now he can definitely help in the contest."

Carissa chuckled. "Have you picked out what you're going to make for the competition?"

"Yes."

"And? What is it?"

"A secret."

"All right, don't tell me." Carissa put her hands up, relenting.

"Is Mr. O'Brien really awake?" Maren asked.

They began tidying up the shop, and Carissa filled her in with the details. The morning went on with business as usual, a fact for which Cari felt grateful and relieved. Noticing that they were out of ginger root tea, Carissa went to the back room to restock. She rummaged through the shelves until she found a pack of half a dozen boxes. Then she turned to leave. The package of teas flew out of her hands as she was startled by a figure sitting in the chair by the computer, facing her. Apparently, Alden didn't need to be in his skeletal form to scare her half to death.

"What are you doing here?" she whispered, bending to retrieve the fallen boxes.

"I'm sorry, I didn't mean to scare you." He stood from his seat and picked up a box, handing it to her. "I've already been to see Cameron, but he wouldn't listen."

"Listen to what?"

He paused. "You remember that MacLir asked whether I took the old ankou to the world beyond?"

"Yes. You said you did."

"I thought I had."

"Thought you had? What do you mean by that?"

"The old ankou. I'm not sure that he's in the world beyond."

"You took him there, didn't you?"

"He followed me into that realm, yes, and he seemed to have lost his grounding to this world as MacLir said he would."

Carissa shook her head. "Then I don't understand. What's the problem?"

"Something he said when I tried to return and couldn't. He said he was grounded more strongly to this world than I am."

"Macara said you were grounded to this world through your mission as ankou."

He waved a hand to disagree. "I never wanted that mission, but even so, MacLir changed the rules of the Otherworld in Moss Hill. I'm bound here by the branch and chalice."

Cari bit her lip. This was too much to take in. "What is MacLir? I know the sidhe are powerful, but what kind of fae can make rules for the Otherworld?"

"He's not fae at all. At least, he's not the kind we're used to."

"Then what is he?"

Alden put a hand on his forehead. After what seemed like an internal debate, he revealed, "He's a Tuatha de Danann. They're known as the Daoine Maithe."

"The Good People." Cari gasped even as she translated the title. The Good People were considered the first of the faeries, the ones from whom modern fae folk had descended. If they were still alive, they were even older than the sidhe and far more powerful. "But they've all gone," Cari said.

"Not all. At least, not him."

"So, he watches over the Otherworld?"

"The gates to it, anyway. He usually chooses a soul who died at the end of a year to be ankou for the next year and then allows them to pass on, but in Moss Hill, he's reserved that fate to only one family."

"The MacAirts," Carissa said.

Alden nodded. "He said that as the current ankou, I was grounded to the world already through the branch and chalice. Unless I'm not the current ankou. If my grandfather was still grounded here somehow, my grasp on this world would have been weakened."

Carissa put the boxes down on the desk. She took a moment to think. "MacLir and Macara seemed to be testing Jane. Do you think MacLir did something on purpose to keep you there so he could test her?"

He looked down. "Maybe." Then he met her eyes with conviction. "But I don't think that's it. My grandfather was smiling when I left him in the void. He fought me at the castle and then he just gave up when we got to the world beyond. It was too easy, but then when I tried to return, I couldn't. It has to be because this world already had an ankou—him. If he's grounded here more firmly than I am, then something is keeping him here."

"What did MacLir say?"

"He said 'so many things bind people together, who's to say what kept me there or what might keep him here.'"

"Are you sure he's here?"

"I can't be sure, but I think so."

Carissa frowned. "Several Mossies were saying that they'd seen the ankou the night of the decorating. Do you think we'll need to cancel the celebration?"

Alden put a hand to his head, ruffling the thick, silky hair he had in this form. "I don't know. He's not bound to the castle like the redcap was. He could be anywhere."

"But he was there," Cari said.

"Yes, over a week ago, but it might've been because he was trying to avoid me. He wanted to stay in this world longer."

Cari leaned against the desk, arms folded with her fingers curled around her chin. Alden kept a hand on his forehead, his face long and solemn.

No wonder Cameron hadn't known what to do. Even she was at a loss. All she could think about was the strange magic on O'Brien.

"Do you think your grandfather might be linked with O'Brien's fall?"

"It's possible, though I don't see why he'd hurt him."

Carissa recalled the wills.

"They were vying for the same estate," Carissa explained about MacAirt inheriting the castle from Eamon O'Brien's father.

"My grandfather never cared to keep Fairfield. He thought it belonged to all of Moss Hill. He was fairly adamant about that before he died."

"How did he pass?"

"A boating accident. He drowned at sea, why?"

Carissa didn't know what it meant yet, but she said, "O'Brien was presumed dead the same way. Seems like an odd coincidence."

Alden shared the look of realization.

"I remember that," he said. "I remember thinking that was strange." His face contracted deeper into concentration.

"What is it?" Carissa inquired.

"I can't remember. I don't remember why, but I know I thought it was strange at the time."

"Worth looking into?"

"You mean following O'Brien? I'm on it." Alden disappeared before her eyes.

Chapter 18

Chaos and Candy Apples

"He's suing me." Cameron's voice rang out as he entered the Seelie Tree Apothecary in the afternoon two weeks after O'Brien's recovery. He'd been so busy with final preparations for the celebration, Cari had hardly spoken to him about anything but All Hallows' Eve. Alden was nearly the same. He'd found no evidence of anything untoward about O'Brien. Cam's news today changed that. His shoulders sulked, and he sounded miserable. He was maybe even more frightened than when they fought the redcap a week prior.

Coming up to the back counter, Cam handed Carissa a paper. The top of the page had the letterhead of Smith and CuCullen Law Firm, but the plaintiff listed in the first paragraph was a Mossie.

"Mr. O'Brien?"

"He says I caused his fall. And it's not just me. He's dragged the mayor into this. He says that 'it's not beyond reason' that the mayor and I conspired to get him out of the way so that we could do whatever we wanted with the castle."

"That's crazy." Maren appeared beside them, holding a basket of herbal supplements she was supposed to be stocking three aisles down. "He can't really believe it."

"There's more," Cameron said. "He met with the mayor this morning with a proposal."

"What?" Maren walked over to the counter so that the three of them were huddled together.

"Shouldn't you be attending to customers?" Carissa asked.

"They're fine." Maren waved off her concern.

Cam lowered his voice, aware now of the two people at the bookcases in the front of the shop. This close to lunchtime, he probably hadn't expected any customers at all.

"He said his memory was fuzzy about whether I caused the fall on purpose or by accident, but that he'd forget the whole thing if we agreed to stop any renovations. He'll even let the celebrations go on as long as they stay in the areas already renovated."

"Isn't that good?" Maren asked. Cam looked at her like she was crazy.

"Don't you see what he's done? He's waited until it's too late to change the plans for the celebration and is using the castle as ransom to get what he wants."

"He doesn't own the castle, not technically," Cari pointed out. "He can't put stipulations on it."

"Haven't you heard?" Cam's tone dripped with sarcasm. "He's next of kin to the late George O'Brien. Without a will, the estate goes to him. Isn't that grand how that all worked out?"

Maren set the basket of supplements on the counter. "All right, the whole thing is bad, but he could do a lot worse. Maybe you can't rebuild the castle, but you can still hold celebrations, and maybe you can convince him to allow tourists in the renovated areas. He's not asking all that much."

"Maren, he's accused me of attempted murder!" He struggled to keep his voice at a whisper.

"Or just negligence," Maren offered unhelpfully.

"Ooh, Parker's going to love this. He'll be the first to say that I ought to be removed from my position."

Carissa cleared her throat as Mr. and Mrs. Reed walked up to the counter. She processed the payment for their items.

Cam went right around the corner to the stool and dragged it to the counter, putting his head in his hands. Maren grabbed the broom, pretending to sweep the floor. She may have actually been cleaning, but Cari knew her well enough to suspect she wasn't. Besides, she was supposed to be restocking. Cari eyed the supplements at the edge of the counter, but Maren didn't catch the hint. Once the Reeds, who at least pretended they hadn't heard their conversation, were out the door, Maren followed them and clicked the lock shut.

"So, what are we going to do about this?" Maren asked.

Cam gave Carissa a pitiful look.

"Okay," Cari said. "Let's just take a step back."

Cam stood as if taking her literally.

"What do we know?" Carissa asked.

"We know Cam definitely didn't push Mr. O'Brien," Maren suggested.

Cam brought his eyebrows together and held out his hands, shaking his head. "Why would you even say that? Of course, I didn't push him."

"All right," Cari broke up the argument she saw coming. "What we know is that O'Brien really doesn't want anyone in the section of the castle that's still in ruins."

"Why not?" Maren asked.

"That's what we need to find out," Carissa said.

"We'd need a warrant. Without one, we'd be breaking the contract. Besides that, there's preparation for the festival over the next few days. We couldn't get in without being seen."

"You're right—if we tried to get inside. But what if it wasn't us?"

"Cari, you can't go in by yourself. It might be dangerous," Cam said.

Cari smirked. "Thanks for your concern, but I wasn't talking about going in by myself. We happen to know someone who can slip in without being seen." Carissa held her eyes on Cam, waiting for him to catch her meaning.

She didn't want to say the name aloud. Maren had seen the ankou before but hadn't yet caught on that it was Alden or that he was actually the ankou and not just a druid with extraordinary ability.

"You're talking about that druid, aren't you?"

Cam's eyes lit in recognition, finally. "Oh, Al-, uh, right, Al." Cam caught himself, changing the pronunciation and shortening the name before he revealed it in front of Maren.

"Al? Seems like an odd name for a druid." Maren pursed her lips. She soon shook it off, sweeping for real this time.

It wasn't that Carissa wanted to keep secrets from Maren, it was that Maren had a penchant for slipping secrets. There was also a part of Cari that felt the less her friend and assistant knew, the better it would be for her if more dark faeries attacked.

Maren refused to leave for lunch without them, which meant that Cari and Cam couldn't call on Alden to investigate. Cameron agreed to pick Maren and Carissa up after work. The hours ticked away slowly.

***

On the grounds, Carissa was too busy with preparations to sneak away and summon Alden. Her position as leader of the decoration committee and Cameron's role as head of the whole event meant that their entire night was taken up by giving directions and taking questions from those involved in the last-minute preparations. The way the evening was turning out, she wouldn't have a chance to summon Alden until the very end.

An hour in, much to both Cam and Carissa's dismay, Mr. O'Brien showed along with the mayor. The two were speaking amiably as far as Cari could tell. How Belkin could laugh and smile with a man who would have accused him of nearly killing him, Carissa couldn't understand. But Mrs. O'Brien was with them, and Cari didn't have the heart to begrudge her. She hugged her upon seeing her.

"Cari, I'm so happy to see him out and about like this. I told him to stay home, but he insisted he was strong enough."

"Mary?" Patsy Harbridge walked up behind her. "Is that you? How is your husband doing?"

"He looks quite well. Doesn't he look much better, Cari?" Mrs. Alcott asked. Wherever Mrs. Harbridge was, rest assured Mrs. Alcott was never far behind.

"Yes, he's back on his feet." Cari tried to sound cheery but couldn't bring herself to say anything more positive than that.

Before long, the two had Mrs. O'Brien in full conversation. Carissa spied Jane Everly on the other side of the courtyard where the haunted house was being set up. Cari had been standing by the gate and missed her, probably because of her preoccupation with the O'Briens. With Mr. O'Brien there, she knew it was a dangerous game she was playing, but she broke away from the group with the excuse of having to check the signs on the attractions.

She pulled Jane aside. The startled girl clasped Cari's forearm.

"What's wrong?" Jane asked.

"Not a thing." Carissa faked a smile in a way that fooled no one. At least, it wouldn't fool anyone eyeing her as carefully as Jane was doing. Cari let go of her breath and relaxed.

"All right, something. But try not to let on."

Jane managed a pleasant half-hearted smile. Given her shy demeanor, it passed as normal for her. Carissa tried to speak in low tones so as not to be overheard.

"You have to summon your brother."

"What, here? Why?"

"Somewhere away from the crowd."

"I'm not sure that's wise."

"It probably isn't, but it may be necessary. Have him—"

An inquisitive sign painter walked toward them, requiring Cari to do her job. At least the cover she'd used to come over here was legitimate after that interruption. Once the volunteer was satisfied with the answer to her question, she left Cari to finish her sentence.

"Have him go to the ruins and search them."

"What for?"

"Anything suspicious, anything that looks like something Mr. O'Brien would rather have covered up."

"Miss Shae," Cari flinched upon hearing Mr. O'Brien call her name. Thankfully, he appeared not to have caught them talking about him in hushed tones seconds earlier.

Carissa slowly made a half-circle with her feet, bringing her face to face with O'Brien and the mayor. The mayor spoke first.

"Marvelous job, Carissa! You and the volunteers have set up the most beautiful displays. I especially like the black field of flowers. How did you do it?"

Carissa politely joked, "Oh, you know, a little magic." She immediately regretted her words. Right beside O'Brien, Reginald Smith decided to make his sneak appearance.

To Cari's surprise, he didn't seem to take her comment literally. "It's very nicely done," he said. Instead of pushing his glasses up from the middle, he touched two fingers to the edge and lifted. It was a much more elegant gesture than she was used to seeing from him.

"Thank you," Cari said. She tried not to look suspicious of the compliment but was very much taken aback by it.

"She saves the day once again." Mr. O'Brien smiled. "Tomorrow's festival is certain to go smoothly, thanks to your contribution."

Cari looked away, making distrust look like humility.

"Don't forget your own contribution," the mayor said. "Your generous allowance for the use of the castle makes it all the more festive a celebration."

This buttery speech was too rich for Carissa to digest.

"Excuse me," she said, "I have a lot to attend to."

"Don't let us keep you," Mr. O'Brien said.

She could feel Reginald's eyes follow her as she left and she shuddered despite herself. She threw one last meaningful look in Jane's direction before leaving. Jane nodded, assuring her that she would do what Cari had asked.

Remedy and Ruins

Hours of preparation passed in the blink of an eye. Carissa hardly noticed the time, except that her aching feet and back seemed to keep a more accurate track of time than her conscious mind did. She and Cameron waited for the very last of the volunteers to call it a night and then made one round of the parts of the castle still within limits. There didn't seem to be anyone around.

Cautiously, she and Cam left the acceptable areas to the ones that were waiting behind the ribbon. She herself had directed the volunteers to set up the yellow tape that read: *Caution: keep out.* Cam lifted the paper barrier for her to duck under. Deeper into the ruins, she and Cameron saw Alden with Jane.

"Did you find anything?" Cam asked.

Carissa found something in the scene in front of her right away that disturbed her. A little nature faerie sat on Alden's shoulder.

"Chaos!" Carissa chided. She couldn't believe her eyes. "What on earth did you do to get all this way here?"

"I brought her," Alden admitted.

"You? What made you think stopping off to get a nature faerie could possibly be a good idea?"

"But she summoned him," Jane said.

"Summoned him?" Cari repeated.

Chaos, swinging her legs and smiling innocently, gave no indication that she had the power to do such a thing. She stared at the sprite in awe. Cameron snapped her out of her shock, repeating his question.

"So, what did you find?"

"Nothing. I can feel something is off on the grounds, but I don't know what," Alden answered.

"Perhaps if we knew what we were looking for," Jane pointed out.

"I don't know, anything suspicious," Cari said.

"It all just looks like debris." Jane frowned.

"If we did find anything, we didn't have a warrant anyway." Cam shrugged. "Maybe it's just as well. The mayor seems to think everything is fine."

He was putting on a brave face, but Cari knew how deeply it hurt him for anyone to hold even a shadow of a doubt that he had attempted murder on a Mossie. She wrapped an arm around him for support.

"We'll keep looking," Alden said.

Chaos pointed to Carissa. When they all failed to understand, she stabbed her index finger out in front of her repeatedly.

"Me? What? Why are you pointing at me?" Cari asked.

"Maybe what we need is fae magic. If there's anything suspicious here, a fae spell might draw it out," Alden reasoned.

"Or a druid one." Jane clasped her hands together. "I'm new at this, but I can ask Macara."

"Or you can get Varick," Alden suggested. "You already know he's trustworthy."

Jane looked down at the ground. Alden didn't seem to notice the pink rising in her face.

"He'll have to attend the celebrations," Cam said. "The sidhe guard will be expected to watch over the event. I can ask him to look into things then."

"If the sidhe is going to be attending…." Carissa began.

"I'll be here," Alden assured. Cari attempted a smile but ended up pulling her lips tightly to one side. Even Cam knew he was taking a risk.

"Thank you," Cameron said softly. "All of you."

"Of course." Jane offered a faint smile.

Alden didn't say anything, but his lips upturned in the same expression as his sister's.

"Come on," Cari said. "Let's get out of here."

Since no one was there, Alden walked with Jane. Cam had offered her a ride so not even Fudge would be waiting outside to see them. The moment they were back in the common area, Chaos's jaw dropped. She'd spotted the sign for the Gooseberry Baking Contest where the table was set up for the next day's event. Stretching her black wings, she took to the air.

"No, Chaos." Cari put a hand around her. "It's not even open right now."

Chaos pouted the whole way home.

Chapter 19
Dark Nights and Dark Fae

Moonlight fell over the castle in an eerie hue. It was the final touch needed for the preparations that had taken up most of the day. The hustle and bustle of volunteers setting up was replaced by the excited chatter of incoming guests.

Children crowded around the attractions like faeries to flowers. Chaos rushed immediately for the sweets. Since it was a celebration, Cari didn't stop her. She'd limit it to a reasonable number, but that was an argument better left to the end of the night. Hiya and Cynth fluttered about somewhere, but their love of sweets was not nearly as strong as Chaos's.

Carissa's concern wasn't the nature faeries. Her eyes scanned the crowd for Cameron or Jane. Holding one of Maren's fresh baked pies in her hand, she leaned this way and that, giving her friend a heart attack.

"Watch the pie!" Maren rushed up behind her and grabbed the confection from her hands. "You'll drop it the way you're swerving. Who are you looking for anyway?"

"No one," Cari said, right as her eyes landed on Cam.

Maren, following her line of sight, murmured, "Mmhm," before taking her leave to set up at Gooseberry's contest table.

Clancy followed behind with his pumpkin carving. He'd done a more than an enviable job on the ghostly face. Barnaby called it "The Face of the Ankou." Cari could've agreed if she hadn't known the specter personally.

"It'll be fine," Barnaby quelled the two nervous contestants. "You've both done marvelous work. Your entries are sure to win!"

Carissa took three steps away from the group and asked Cam, "Have you seen Varick yet?"

Cam shook his head. He shot his eyes sideways. The mayor emerged behind him, followed by O'Brien.

"A fine job," Belkin put his arm on Cameron's shoulder, "and you, too, Cari. I'd say it's going splendidly."

"What were you saying about Varick?" Mr. O'Brien crossed his arms, putting one hand to his chin. "Is that a fae name? It sounds like one."

"He's a friend," Cam said quickly. "Cari has friends from Vale attending."

As if on cue, Hela's voice chimed through the air, "Carissa! Oh, everything looks fantastic!" The elf woman rushed up to them.

"So, this is a human celebration of All Hallows' Eve," Sal observed. His wide eyes took in everything: the apple bobbing, food stalls, pumpkin carvings, ghostly bounce house, carnival games, and the section of the main castle that was open for a haunted house, complete with cobwebs everywhere. With such little time to prepare, some of those cobwebs might have been real. "It's remarkable."

"We're looking forward to participating in it," Fen, Hela's husband, said in his natural cordiality.

"I'm glad you like it." Carissa smiled. "May I introduce Mr. O'Brien and, of course, you know Cam and the mayor. This is Hela, daughter of Rolin of Vale, and her husband, Fenigar, son of Orin of Vale. And this is Sal of the Rolin household."

Cari hated introducing Sal that way, but elves took after the sidhe in their strict ranking system. Sal was a servant in their household, so the introduction as such was necessary. Mr. O'Brien didn't seem to notice Sal at all.

"Daughter of Rolin, you say? Head of the Elven Council? Well, I'm delighted to meet you both." He kissed Hela's hand and shook Fen's. Sal gave him the customary bow.

Their arrival cost her twenty minutes of small talk and little time to speak privately with Cameron. The two seconds where she and Cam stepped aside had O'Brien raising an eyebrow. It was like he was purposely keeping tabs on Cam.

"Don't worry," Cari said, "whatever he's hiding, we'll get this solved tonight."

Cam gave her a warning look. "If you don't find Varick, don't go into the ruins alone."

If she'd promised not to, she wouldn't have meant it. Turns out she didn't have a chance to say anything at all. Maren interrupted them, stepping between them frantically, holding a crying Chaos in her hands.

"Oh no," Cari said. "Did she eat too much?"

Cam was called back by the mayor. He gave one final glance at Carissa before disappearing into the crowd.

"It's so much worse! Come here."

Maren grabbed Carissa, still holding Chaos in one hand. Dragging Cari over to the treat tables, she pointed to three blackened apples. The caramel seeped over them, oozing down to a rotten center in each one.

"Chaos did this?"

"She just touched them. She came close to the caramel apples and Mrs. Harbridge waved her away a bit sternly. She said they were for paying customers. I happened to see it, so I stepped in to pay a moment later. Chaos demanded three of them," Maren tilted her head and lowered her voice, "you know how she is. Anyway, I paid and the second Chaos touched them, this is what happened."

Carissa picked one up. It dripped black goo onto the ground. Chaos cried harder and hugged Maren's thumb for comfort.

"Get those out of here." Mrs. Harbridge, who had just finished taking payment and putting it into the cashbox, leaned over the table of sweets and said in a harsh whisper, "You're scaring the customers!"

Carissa and Maren threw the three rotten apples away. Then Cari took Chaos into both hands. She didn't really know what to say.

"It's Okay, we'll take you home to Nan. She might know what to do."

Chaos sniffled and wiped her eyes with her sleeve. She nodded. Poor Chaos must've felt awful. She didn't even argue about staying. At home, she might still enjoy the evening of passing out candies to trick-or-treaters with Nan.

Cari began formulating the plan in her mind. There was no way Maren was volunteering to leave, so she'd have to take Chaos home herself. She could drive back in the car. Technically, Jane or Cam could speak to Varick, but Cam was tied up with the mayor and Jane seemed to be avoiding the sidhe guard lately. Besides that, she had a sense of danger that was growing in the pit of her stomach.

She walked over in time to see Reginald entering the castle gate. She took several pounding steps over to reprimand him for attending a Mossie-only event. Her pace slowed as she saw the determined look on his face. His jaw was rigidly set and stern. His eyes focused in front of him. His glasses, he took them off and cleaned them with a handkerchief he removed from his breast pocket, all without taking his eyes off of the castle ruins.

The movements were fluid and suave—not the awkward confidence of the tourist who'd come to Moss Hill. She traced the path of his attention to the highest window of the castle. It was where Alden had transported them the day of the cleansing.

Curious. It would've made far more sense for Alden to have taken them to the building across from the main castle: the keep. The keep was the tallest building in the entire structure. It had a view of every angle of the castle and was a prime location in which to defend it. But Alden had said that his powers draw him to places. Had they drawn him to that room?

Reginald walked forward, heading straight to the castle ruins. Carissa followed him. Chaos tugged at her ear. She must've noticed the change in direction and wondered what was going on.

"Sorry, Chaos, I have to do this. We can't leave yet."

Reg made his way past the food stalls, the attractions, and the music, into the part of the castle taped off. She joined a line for a mummy bowling game as he looked over the crowd to make sure he wasn't seen. Then, he ducked below the caution tape and disappeared into the building. Carissa stepped out of line to continue her pursuit. Chaos quivered in her hair, pulling at the strands of red. Carissa put a hand to her neck to calm her.

"Shh, it's okay. Go stay with Maren. I'll take you home a little later."

Chaos whacked her with her feet. Carissa tried to grab hold of her, but Chaos jumped away.

"I mean it, Chaos. This could be dangerous." She looked down to see the nature faerie on the edge of her shoulder shaking her head furiously.

"All right. If you're staying with me, stay out of sight. I promise I'll try to do the same."

Cari walked closer and maneuvered under the tape and into the dark hallway. She used her elf-light only from one hand. If Reginald saw her, she could say she had a flashlight. The place had been creepy during the day. It was ten times dustier and had twice as many cobwebs at night. Or, so it seemed.

The shine from her hands lit up the steps. The winding staircase only heightened her fear. She rallied her courage and began the long climb. Around the first bend, her light shown on two glowing eyes.

She gasped.

The eyes became Reginald's natural brown hue, and he beamed a flashlight of his own in her direction. She put her hands up to shield her eyes from the light.

"Cari?" Reg asked.

"Yeah." She let her elf-light fade, hoping he hadn't seen it for what it was. She didn't want to make a hostile move until she was sure he wasn't innocent in all of this. All of what exactly this was had yet to be determined.

"What are you doing here?"

"I could ask you that question, Reg." She waved her hand so he would get the flashlight out of her face. It was a tiny one, but extra bright. He'd come prepared. The question was, for what?

"I'm glad you're here," Reginald said as he turned around and kept walking in the dark. "I don't think I can do this alone."

"Do what?" Carissa asked.

The ominous reply, "You'll see," was all she could get out of him.

Reginald led them farther and farther into the castle, to a door that jammed as they entered. Reg pushed until it swung open. Footprints on the dusty floor revealed that at least three people had been there recently. Cari hoped Reg would miss that. One thing was clear, though. There was no proof that Reginald had been up here before.

"What are we doing here?" Carissa asked.

"I overheard O'Brien speaking," Reginald said. "He murdered a man in this room: Corbin MacAirt."

Cari paused. Alden's grandfather, murdered? She might've gasped except that when she thought about it, that made sense. The barguest only appeared when a prominent person in Moss Hill died. Yet, it had been seen by the castle. People attributed that to the spirits that died in ancient wars on the castle grounds. But now that she thought about it, the dog could've also been drawn there by a more recent murder.

A murder that would have taken place five years ago, around the same time O'Brien left Moss Hill. Cari's mind made the connection between killer and victim.

"O'Brien's father left the castle to his daughter's family, not his son's. She was married to a MacAirt. Eamon couldn't stand the thought of the castle leaving the O'Brien name, so he brought MacAirt here to 'talk.' When he arrived, Eamon walked with him through the castle grounds, pretending to listen to Corbin's plans for renovations and his vision for renewal, but, in this room, he knew that the walls were soundproof.

"He used fae magic, specifically ban sidhe magic, as borrowed from his family's past links to faeries, to kill MacAirt. Then, he used the magic—without knowing how to use it properly—to phase him right into a wall." Reginald put his hand right over a spot in the wall just left of center.

Carissa stepped back. This didn't sound like Reginald anymore.

"How do you know this?" Carissa asked.

"I told you. I overheard it."

She shook her head. "Why would Mr. O'Brien go into such detail?"

Reg stared at her, stoically. "What matters," he dipped his head down, readjusting his glasses again with the tip of his finger, "is that you, with your elf-light, can go into the Otherworld and undo the magic that's keeping the body there."

"Magic? I don't know what you're talking about." Carissa inched her way to the door.

"Yes, you do." His voice became firmer, "The dead need closure, Carissa. This is a chance to unearth a mystery, a chance to expose a murderer for what he really is."

"Then we'll get the police."

Reginald moved with inhuman speed to the door, blocking her path. "They won't believe you. They'll spout things like warrants and probable cause."

"They'll also take your word that you heard him talking about it." Carissa tried to keep her voice steady and her elf-light at bay.

"No, what I need is your magic. That's a far easier way to deal with this."

Chaos was making her warning clear with her fingernails. Carissa understood the warning now.

"There's no way O'Brien shared this information with you, Reginald. You'd have to know this some other way. Who are you?"

Reginald grumbled. "Don't be difficult. All I'm asking for is justice."

Carissa made the final connection. "Justice for yourself or someone else?"

"Now I see why Alden goes to you for help. You do catch on, but not quickly enough." Reg put a hand to his forehead. When his eyes looked back at her again, they were red.

Cari's heart raced and she reflexively stuck her hands out in front of her.

He wasn't listening, he was raising his own hands to attack. Elf-light magic shot from her fingertips to preempt his strike. At first, she felt the stream of light in front of her had hit its target and that Reginald was not attacking nor defending himself.

To her horror, she then realized that he was absorbing her magic. She felt some force pulling at her forward. She tried to fight it, but the more she did, the stronger the pull became.

"No," she uttered in a vain effort at resistance.

Her fear doubled when she saw Chaos fly out from behind her. The brave sprite wasn't even noticed by her attacker. Carissa could see her flying into the stream of magic.

"Stop!" Cari shouted. Reginald laughed, a terrifying chortle that echoed in the empty room. It worked in their favor that he assumed she was yelling at him.

Chaos slipped into the elf-light without him seeing. The yellow light began to turn black. Reg's red eyes widened and his face contorted as he realized something was wrong.

Chaos flung both of her little hands out against the attack. Black light shot out in a blast of energy. Reginald flew back.

But the specter that had possessed him did not. Chaos had cast the spirit from Reg's body. All Cari could do was stare in wonder. Nan had been right. Chaos was full of surprises. With the magic stream done, Carissa felt exhaustion overtake her. She fell to the floor, panting.

"You-you're not Reg. You're...ankou," she managed to say between breaths.

Red fire reflected in the eyes of the skeletal face hovering over her. Her vision blurred. She tried to inch away, but her body reacted sluggishly to her brain's commands. Sprawled on the floor, she tried to stand up, but the movement made her woozy. She put a hand to her head. The figure moved as if to attack.

"Alden!" Carissa cried out.

Her hand shot out in defense, but the action was too much for her.

"Alden, please," she whispered, not knowing if he would hear her, "help."

Dizziness, then darkness, overwhelmed her. The music and the laughter of the All Hallows' Eve celebrations taking place on the other side of the castle drifted into the window. Here, in the half-constructed ruins of the west wing, no one would know she was in danger.

The window was too far for anyone to see her—if anyone was even looking. Why, oh, why hadn't she listened to Cam? Regret formed her final thought before Carissa gave way to unconsciousness.

Then, she dreamed. All the events of the last few days played over again in her mind like a movie, closed captioned on the words "I warned you so" from the imagined face of a woman she'd never met: Ms. Raven Corvus.

Chapter 20

Grim Reaper

Something hit Cari's cheek with enough force for her to drift back to consciousness. Carissa groaned, putting a hand to the back of her head, but a minuscule force kept pouncing on her cheek. Tiny hands and feet—that's what it felt like. When she finally turned her head to figure out that it was Chaos frantically trying to wake her, she closed her eyes in relief. This only made Chaos hit her again.

"I'm awake," Cari responded. Chaos's shoulder hit her jaw. "Ow, I'm awake!"

Carissa sat up, still clutching the back of her head. That was when she saw it: the skeletal specter that had to be an ankou standing too close for comfort. Cari put a hand in front of Chaos, pulling her backward, and she propelled herself to her feet. This caused a wave of dizziness, which made her let go of Chaos and fling an arm backward, hoping to encounter a wall. A hand met hers instead.

"Take it easy, you're okay," a voice said behind her. She swung around.

"Alden!" She flung her arms around him without thinking.

He felt odd in her grip, unnatural. It wasn't just the awkwardness of her sudden reaction. He stood with his arms out, seemingly startled by her. Not feeling him return the hug was only part of why she let go so suddenly. He wasn't warm, he had no breath, she felt no heartbeat. It was like hugging stone.

She took a step back. Her cheeks reddened. Chaos didn't seem to notice or care about Alden's lack of warmth or Carissa's awkwardness. The little faerie hugged Alden's neck and settled happily on his shoulder. His eyes looked down at the sprite fondly as a smile came to his lips.

Carissa turned back toward the specter. Two ankous? One was shock enough. If Cam were here, he'd lose his mind.

"Who are you?" Cari asked the apparition, though she felt she already knew the answer. The specter had the same black hair, the same blue eyes, the same structured jaw as the ankou behind her. Even the see-through, skeletal form was similar.

"He's my grandfather," Alden revealed. There was a sorrow, a gentleness, and a tinge of regret in Alden's voice.

"MacAirt." Cari looked between the two. "So, you're the last ankou?"

Alden's grandfather seemed to hear her unspoken question. "Corbin MacAirt," he introduced himself as if he hadn't just tried to possess her, "of the MacAirts who have served as ankous since the first to encounter Manann MacLir."

Carissa remembered the story Magnus had told her, but even more recently, the one Alden had told about returning him to the world beyond. "So you did escape from the world beyond."

"I was still grounded to my body." MacAirt laughed. "O'Brien knew nothing about magic. He grounded me to him far better than even Jane did for you." He nodded in his grandson's direction.

"But if you've been ankou for years, why not go to the Everly's—to someone—for help? Why not tell them that O'Brien had killed you?"

"Yes, years I've had to ground myself to O'Brien." He seemed to say to himself.

"If no one else could see you, at least I could," Alden said. "Why not just tell me? You could've told me, and we would've made sure O'Brien saw justice."

"Justice? I don't want justice. I want revenge. He deserves to suffer." MacAirt looked at Alden. "You know, you're breaking a rule. No one is supposed to see an ankou. Well, I broke that rule, too, but more to torture a killer than to not allow my friends and family to move on."

"Everyone wondered why O'Brien left Moss Hill. He left because of me—because I haunted him. He couldn't see me as myself, just as the ankou. And I made him miserable."

His smile was savage.

"But O'Brien left," Alden said. "Moss Hill couldn't have gone five years without an ankou."

"I'd have left my post as ankou, if MacLir would've let me, to follow him. I heard the reports of his death. I felt he was alive, but I couldn't be sure. When Alden came for me, I wasn't against leaving, if only to see if O'Brien was already in the world beyond. But O'Brien had returned and so did my hatred for him. I wanted to take him with me. So the red fae did what he does best."

"You brought the redcap here?" Carissa asked.

"No," Alden's grandfather scoffed, "the hobgoblin did that months ago—around the same time he was defeated, I believe. I just persuaded the redcap to choose O'Brien as his next victim."

"But he didn't die. When he was healed, you decided to possess Reginald," Carissa said.

The poor tourist was still lying unconscious on the floor.

"The priest was actually undoing my grounding. Can you believe it? But then all that light energy flying around, especially my own ancestral magic, and this fool was right there. It couldn't have been easier."

They quieted. Footsteps could be heard in the hall. Then a soft voice, "Cari?" It was Jane.

"No!" MacAirt whispered hoarsely. "I didn't want to involve her. I didn't want to involve you, either," he said to Alden.

"That's why you came after me?" Carissa asked. "You needed someone with magic but didn't want it to be Jane."

"Not just *someone with magic*, someone with strong magic. You."

Carissa shook her head. "My magic is not strong."

"It's not *practiced*. It is strong—maybe stronger than even Jane's and she's the most promising druidess since the Morrigan sisters graced this humble town. With your magic, I might not just be able to uncover my old body, I might be able to restore it."

Chaos took to her feet on Alden's shoulder. She posed defensively, as if ready for a fight. The ankou made no attempt to attack.

"I'm afraid even Carissa's magic can't do that," the smooth, rich voice of Magnus MacLir said from the doorway. He turned as a woman entered behind him. "See, my dear? I told you we'd find them."

"Are you all right?" Jane asked. She lifted her elegant black dress and passed MacLir inside.

Alden nodded.

Carissa was surprised she could even find her voice to say "I'm fine" in response.

"Manann, you must let me stay. I have unfinished business," the specter of Corbin MacAirt pleaded.

"Of course, you can stay," he said. "You can watch Jane here uncover your body with her magic. Your flashy fight with the elf-light should've caught the attention of the sidhe guard and the mayor, with a little help from a certain clever lady who told them to look up at just the right moment. Then, once O'Brien is arrested, your 'unfinished business' is finished."

MacAirt looked down, defeated. He didn't argue or make any movement to fight his fate. Alden moved closer to him, preparing just in case.

MacLir held his hand out. "Go on then, Jane."

She took some herbs from a small velvet bag and sprinkled them on the floor. Then, she began her incantation. Light shot from her hand, swirling in a large circle in front of her. Something like a portal seemed to open on the wall.

The opening revealed nothing.

"Carissa," MacLir said, "a little help." He tilted his head toward the empty space. "That—not us," he clarified.

Carissa's hand went to her locket. She knew what he was asking. She uttered the phrase that allowed her to see into both the human and fae worlds at once. With Jane's magic still at work, she could see the remains there in the wall. Turning the circles, she used her elf-magic to transport the body out of the Otherworld into their realm.

Footsteps clomped outside the open door. Three people rushed in. Cameron entered first, followed by the mayor and Mr. O'Brien. Cam rushed to Carissa. He put a hand on her arm.

"Are you al—oh, my gosh. Is that a skeleton?" Cam's comforting gesture turned into a full grip of death.

"Ow, Cam! Let go."

"Sorry." He released his grip. "Who is that?"

At first, she thought he was referring to the ankou MacAirt, but looking toward the window, she saw that he had disappeared, as had Alden. She was sure they wouldn't have left yet but had only cloaked themselves in the presence of others, especially as Reginald was waking.

"What happened?" Reginald said.

Cam looked at Carissa, then went over and helped him up.

"C'mon, Reg, let's get you out of here." He led him out of the room. Carissa hoped he could come up with some viable explanation.

"This is an outrage." O'Brien was both pale and splotched with redness all over his face. "Sneaking to off-limit parts of the castle planting fake skeletons."

"I can personally attest that we saw a light, which brought us here and discovered the body only seconds before you arrived."

The sidhe guard pushed their way past the spectators. The mayor and O'Brien stepped helplessly aside.

"Have you touched anything?" Varick knelt beside the corpse.

"No," Carissa spoke for the group.

Varick and his guards conducted their interrogation for what felt like hours. The guards' magic on the wall led to one conclusion.

"This was murder," Varick finally said. "Murder by magic."

Cari bit her lip. They still had nothing to tie the murder to O'Brien. Perhaps they would find something in the rubble, or maybe Varick could talk to the ankou MacAirt one last time before he left this world.

Carissa looked at MacLir. He only smiled and gave a subtle back and forth with his chin. That was a no. Why was he so adamant about MacAirt not being seen?

Still able to see into the Otherworld, Carissa stepped forward. There was something else in the wall, with MacAirt. She couldn't make out exactly what it was, but it was small, black, and leather. She squinted and turned the locket, focusing on it. Varick traced her eyeline to where an object materialized before him. It was small a book of spells that had tumbled from the skeleton's hands.

Varick picked it up. He opened the first page. His eyes widened, and immediately he turned on O'Brien.

"Under suspicion of murder, you, Eamon O'Brien, are under arrest."

The guards surrounded Mr. O'Brien.

"This is a mistake," Mr. O'Brien said. "Do something, Belkin!" His face reddened and sweat beads formed on his forehead.

"Well, I, wait a minute," the mayor was flustered. "On what grounds are you basing his arrest?"

"What was in the notebook?" MacLir asked. Carissa had the sneaking suspicion that he knew. She had a feeling he knew everything that was unfolding.

Varick answered by holding the book up. It was a symbol on the first page, the symbol of a cat with glowing eyes. "The family seal of the O'Briens of Moss Hill, and the will to the Fairfield estate," Varick said.

"That's mine," O'Brien exclaimed. He lunged for the book. Varick took one slick step and caught his arm, pinning it to his back.

"That book is the property of Fairfield and Fairfield is mine," O'Brien howled like a wild man.

Varick conjured handcuffs to the old man's wrist.

"You'll regret this. I've made friends with people more powerful than you can imagine. You cannot just arrest me like this!"

"You'll have a trial," Varick said, "with the Sidhe Council of Elders."

O'Brien paled.

Chapter 21

All Hallows' Eve Celebrations

Maren's cheeks turned red. The rest of the crowd might've thought it was anxiety, but Carissa knew full well that she was holding her breath. Maren's nervous, hope-filled eyes met Cari's, and she gave her friend a thumbs up as they waited for the Gooseberry's booth to announce the winner of the baking contest.

"Ladies and gentlemen, guys and ghouls, this year's Gooseberry baking champions are.... Maren Raines and Clarence of Vale for their delicious pumpkin pecan pie!"

Carissa clapped loudly for her friends. Maren and Clancy walked around the table so the woman in the red Gooseberry shirt could hand them their ribbons. Chaos twirled through the air. Faerie dust sparkled around her. Cari saw her wings clearly for the first time just then.

"Chaos," she said, "your wings, they're back to normal."

Chaos looked behind her, curling her wings forward so she could see them. The sight of it evoked a joyful reaction. She spun even farther up and around the entire crowd, sprinkling faerie dust everywhere. Hiya and Cynth took note from wherever they were wandering around, for soon there were three nature faeries, then more, dancing overhead.

Cari laughed, and the crowd gasped in awe. The Mossies knew it was the nature faeries among them, especially the fae attendees. Carissa hoped that Reginald, if he saw this, thought that it was glitter or some other special effect.

She hugged Maren and congratulated her once she came away from the table, wearing a bright orange #1 ribbon pinned to her dress. Chaos was only interested in the pies being sliced up now for guests at the Gooseberry table. She floated over to a little girl holding a much too large slice for herself and licked her lips. Making the cutest face she was capable of, with large eyes, upraised eyebrows, and an innocent smile, Chaos clasped her hands hopefully. Her eyes wandered over the table and back to the little girl in the princess dress.

"You can share my slice," the girl offered. Chaos lifted a long napkin and tucked it into the collar of her orange dress. It draped way past her little frame, which was good, because the way she devoured the pie, pumpkin and pecan flew everywhere.

Maren was too excited to yell at Chaos for demolishing her masterpiece. "Guess what? The owner of Gooseberry was so impressed by my pie, she asked if I could bake for the shop!"

Carissa's face fell.

"Just on special occasions," Maren quickly added. "It'd be a side job, something I could do when I'm not working at the Seelie Tree."

Cari's alarmed expression settled back to normal. She tried to smile but had a gnawing feeling that Maren may have found something she loved better than the apothecary shop. As happy as she was for her friend, she was a little sad for herself.

"I'm glad for you, Maren. I hope that it works out well." And she meant it.

"Ladies and gentlemen," the announcer from the Gooseberry table said into the microphone. "We have the winner of the pumpkin carving contest. It's Emony of Vale for her *Cat Sidhe* pumpkin."

A woman at the Gooseberry booth placed the pumpkin in the center of the table. The carving of a cat with sharp teeth and mischievous eyes stared at the crowd. It glowed from a candle placed in the center of the pumpkin. The crowd clapped as a brownie about the same height at Clancy received her ribbon.

Clancy and Maren joined Carissa now that the contest was over. Giving Maren a hug, she congratulated her and Clarence for their win.

"And I'm sorry you didn't win the pumpkin carving portion of the contest as well," Cari added.

"Who says I lost?" Clancy took off his cap and smoothed his hair. "If you'll excuse me, a certain lady is waiting for me. I'm sorry, Maren, it just wouldn't have worked out."

He strutted off toward Emony. The two fae folk flaunted their medallions to the crowd. Barnaby shook his cousin's hand. Clancy beamed with pride.

"Well, that was the oddest breakup I've ever had," Maren joked.

"Don't take it too hard." Cari patted her back, pretending to soothe her for the loss of the one-sided relationship.

From the corner of her eye, Carissa spotted Jane and Macara in the pathway between the spider ring toss and the monster face painting booth. Cari excused herself and walked over to the two.

"How's your brother?" she asked Jane, mindful to keep her voice low as the rest of Moss Hill was unaware of his ankou status.

"He's fine. He's taken our grandfather back to the world beyond."

Jane's stoic face told her nothing as to which one, justice or mercy, MacAirt would encounter in the world beyond.

Carissa put a hand on Jane's shoulder. "I'm sorry you had to go through any of this."

Jane's hand rested on her pendant. The tree emblem reflected a subtle glow in the moonlight. "This was supposed to happen. I've been fighting my destiny."

Macara stepped up beside her, wrapping an arm around her shoulder. "She'll do very well. And so, I dare say, shall you."

Jane looked across the courtyard to where Varick's guards not so discreetly pushed a handcuffed Mr. O'Brien through a stunned crowd. The mayor's hands hushed the people.

"It's all right. Move on. Keep enjoying the festivities. Everything's fine." Mayor Belkin took a handkerchief from the inside of his jacket pocket and wiped the sweat off his brow.

"Mr. Varick," Carissa heard Belkin say as they passed by, "could you not be less obvious about this? Your guards could at least walk along the side of the wall instead of pushing through the middle of the events!"

Varick spun on his heel and stopped. He was a full head taller than the mayor, who was not a short man, and fearsome when the sparks of gold glimmered in his eyes. Mayor Belkin shriveled under his stare. He withdrew his complaint.

"Of course, you're welcome to do whatever you think is best."

Varick made as if to turn and halted as his vision encountered Jane. Carissa had never seen him hesitate like that. He opened his mouth as if to speak. Jane turned and walked into the crowd. Macara made a gesture to pull her back, but she held a hand up. Macara stopped and closed her eyes, nodding. She may not have agreed with Jane's decision to leave, but she wouldn't argue with her.

Macara's eyes landed on Carissa next. She took a breath. She knew what Macara wanted her to do.

"Varick," she caught the sidhe guard before he turned around. She rummaged through her purse and retrieved a note from it. It was a little crinkled from how many times she'd read it over. She had it memorized by now.

"I received this note a while back. I think the Sidhe Council should be informed of it."

Varick took the note from her hands. He read it over. By the time he'd finished his eyes were solid gold. "A while back?" he asked.

"Four months ago," Carissa admitted.

The sidhe guard glowered. "You should not have kept this from us."

Carissa bit her tongue. She wanted to shout back that she tried but they would barely listen to her months ago. Except for Varick himself, the sidhe were still impossible to talk to. Her cheeks reddened as he folded the note and placed it carefully into his notepad. Without another word, he walked away.

When Cari regained enough composure not to be deafened by the pulse of her own heart, she could hear Reginald enter the area. She turned to see the tourist with Cameron at his heels. Reg was beside himself.

"Elves and leprechauns," he was explaining to Cam, "and I don't even know what she is." He pointed to a dryad. The slight green hue of the tree faerie might be slightly accentuated by the moonlight, but she was human enough as she ate her cotton candy and laughed with a group of Mossies. "If only I had my camera."

"It's not what you think," Cameron tried to explain. "It's just costumes. Or, I guess you believe that's really a pumpkin?"

He pointed out a dog dressed in a cute pumpkin outfit with a little stem and leaf hat set atop its head.

Fortunately for him, several residents were in costume for the festival, which lent itself well to his explanation, even if his example wasn't the best one. Reginald wasn't buying it.

"You can try to hide it all you want, but I *know* this is Hy Brasil." Several heads from the crowd turned to Reg. Murmurs began among the fae folk. The mention of the place seemed to provoke an unsettling reaction.

Magnus MacLir walked up to Cari.

"Someone will have to set that boy straight."

Carissa nodded. "He's liable to tell everyone about Moss Hill."

"He's trying too hard to impress you. If he keeps on like that, he'll either end up mayor or die trying to get you to notice him."

"Reginald?" Carissa's voice piqued as high as her surprise.

Magnus, who was really Manann, tilted his head. He held that same chiding look Carissa often gave to Cam when he wasn't understanding. Suddenly, she understood. He meant Cameron. Cari looked away, changing the subject.

"Why did everyone look scared? Are they afraid that he'll expose Moss Hill as Hy Brasil?" Carissa asked.

"Hy Brasil is not a land of fae folk, but of people far more powerful."

"The Tuatha de Danann: The Good People?"

MacLir smiled but wouldn't answer. Cari stared him down. He wouldn't budge.

"You are Manann MacLir, though? The same one from the legend?"

"Are any of us the same after so many years?"

The man was infinitely frustrating. She wouldn't let him get around her questions so easily.

She looked him directly in the eye. "I knew a woman who said you killed her husband-to-be."

He considered her carefully. "You are fearless. That's commendable. No, she was mistaken. I've never taken a life without returning it, except maybe one."

Carissa's eyes flared. Did he just admit to murder? "Whose?" she asked.

He breathed in. "No, not commendable, necessary. Carissa, you will need your fearlessness in the coming months more than you realize. You don't know what you've done giving that note to the sidhe. It was a mistake you'll need to be ready to pay the consequence for."

So, he wasn't going to answer her question. She debated telling the mayor about his admission. But then, what jurisdiction did they have over something that might have happened centuries ago? Maybe the sidhe were the right authorities to go to. But he was telling her not to go them, even about the note.

"Macara said it was necessary," Carissa argued.

"Oh, yes, it was necessary," he agreed, to her surprise, "but it was also a mistake."

"Why?"

"Because it means you'll be getting your answer about Hy Brasil very soon." He put his hand out in the air. A swirl of blue light danced around his fingers and the golden chalice appeared in his hand. Carissa looked around, hoping no tourist had been nearby. Reginald was still being distracted by Cameron.

"I think you may find a use for this at some point."

"But that belongs to the Everlys," she argued.

"Not at all. It belongs to me."

She warily took the cup into her hands. "You said it restores people 'among other things.' What else can this goblet do?"

He winked, as if that was some sort of response, and made his way over to Cameron and Reginald. She stood there, holding the golden cup in shock. She had a sinking feeling in her gut that by accepting it, she'd just signed up for more trouble.

"How would you like a job, young man?" she heard him say as he put a hand on Reg's shoulder. "I could use a person like you."

Carissa quickly concealed the cup in her purse, though she couldn't take her eyes off the odd pair as she did so. In her periphery, Cari spied Parker approaching Cam. She couldn't miss that conversation and so decided a little more elfish eavesdropping was in order. She watched from a distance.

"Turns out I was wrong about you," Parker extended a hand. "My apologies."

Cam hesitated. That wasn't quite a heartfelt acknowledgment of his error, but Cameron truly was the better man. He accepted the handshake with a friendlier reply than Carissa might've given him.

"It's all right," Cam said. "No harm done."

He put his hand on the back of his head as Parker left. He always did that when he felt awkward about something. His eyes shifted to her. This time, she didn't care that he'd seen her. She shared a smile with him. He blushed. That was the Cameron she knew.

"What was that all about?" Carissa's face reddened this time. She looked down to see Barnaby with a hot chocolate in hand, but he was not focused on her exchange with Cam.

The leprechaun was sipping and watching the mayor consoling Mrs. O'Brien and batting away questions from Mrs. Harbridge and Mrs. Alcott. The ladies would not stop without a full explanation.

"It's a long story, Barnaby," Carissa said. She spotted Tilly listening in on Mayor Belkin's explanation. "I'm sure you'll read all about tomorrow," Cari said. Though, it would be a non-magical version now that Tilly understood that the World Wide Web was not the place to share the secrets of Moss Hill. "How's Clancy?" she asked the leprechaun.

"He's well, much better now." He tipped his cup at his clurichaun cousin, who was timidly tasting the warm chocolatey drink. He put it to his lips, sipping once, then twice. A smile spread across his face, and he drank a mouthful then wiped his chin.

"He's very grateful to you, Carissa, for believing in his innocence."

"I knew he wasn't guilty."

"He's not a bad guy, you know, underneath it all. Most people don't know him well enough to see that."

"If he comes to more events like this, the people of Moss Hill will get to know him eventually."

"Cari—" Maren interrupted. "The sprites are getting cold. I think the night is getting too chilly for them.

"Bye, Barn," Carissa said, then, turning to her friend, she smiled at the three shivering faeries. "Come on, let's get the sprites home."

She, Maren, and the three nature faeries walked past all the Mossies still celebrating together. She heard Mrs. Alcott as she passed.

"On my faith, this was a nasty ankou."

She meant it, of course, in the traditional sense of the phrase. It meant it was a harsh year for losing loved ones or dealing with death. She was right, of course, but she didn't know just how right she was.

MacAirt had been a nasty ankou. But, looking up at the shadowy figure in the tower watching over the people of Moss Hill this All Hallows' Eve, she knew this one was different. With MacLir's warning of more troublesome times ahead, she was glad he would be there with them.

Chaos tugged at Carissa's earring. She looked down. The sprite was motioning with her hands cupped, pretending to drink. "Sure, Chaos, we'll get you all some tea."

Chaos's eyes widened and her hands lifted in a palms-up questioning style. Carissa knew what she was asking: *What kind of tea?* She also knew the answer the sprite was looking for.

She gave a heartfelt laugh, replying, "Why, pumpkin spice, of course."

Want more great content?

Hi, I'm Astoria Wright, the author of The Faerie Apothecary Cozy Mysteries. I hope you've enjoyed the first book in this series.

Check out the rest of
The Faerie Apothecary Mysteries:

Chaos in the Countryside – A Novella Prequel
Book 1: *Herbs and Homicide*
Book 2: *Remedy and Ruins*
Book 3: *Elixirs and Elves* (December 2018)
Book 4: *Charms and Changelings* (February 2019)
Book 5: *Potions and Panic* (May 2019)
Book 6: *Talismans and Turmoil* (October 2019)
Book 7: *Tonics and Turning Points* (December 2019)

To keep up to date about this series and others by the author, check out the website:

www.astoriawright.com

Sign up for the mailing list for updates and freebies available only to members!

A Note from Chaos:

Do you like this book?
I hope you do.
Please do me a favor
and leave a review!
(on Amazon)

Thanks for reading!